"You're really something, Rebecca."

He looked up at her, silhouetted against the sharp blue sky. Her expression became serious as their gazes held. Time stilled, and it seemed as if the world had condensed down to the two of them.

She matters so much to me, Joe thought. I love her.

He shook his head as the thought settled. Yesterday, up in the hills, it seemed easy to imagine the possibility, to indulge in the notion. But here, on his own small place, it seemed suddenly remote.

Was he being foolish? Overshooting himself? What did he have to offer any woman, let alone one like Rebecca? A run-down ranch and a pile of debts? He glanced at Rebecca, who looked at him in puzzlement, and in spite of his questions, Joe felt his heart lift as their eyes met once more.

Maybe it would work....

Books by Carolyne Aarsen
Love Inspired

CAROLYNE AARSEN

"Once upon a time" are four words that still have the ability to bring a sense of expectation to Carolyne Aarsen. It is the same wonder at the world God has given us and the people that live in it that fires her imagination and daydreams.

Her husband, a man of many talents, built a little cabin in the woods, a few hundred feet away from the house, with a view of trees and that endless Alberta sky. It was meant for guests, but she has taken it over for writing.

Through all of her stories, Carolyne wishes to portray how God has worked in her own life and in the life of her family and community. She wants to show people's weaknesses and Christ's strength. Her dream is to make Christ's sacrifice accessible to people of all ages and places by making people laugh, cry or sigh.

The Cowboy's Bride
Carolyne Aarsen

Love Inspired™

Published by Steeple Hill Books™

STEEPLE HILL BOOKS

Steeple
Hill™

ISBN 0-373-87067-1

THE COWBOY'S BRIDE

Copyright © 1999 by Carolyne Aarsen

Visit us at www.steeplehill.com

Printed in U.S.A.

But seek first His kingdom and His righteousness and all these things will be given to you as well. Therefore, do not worry about tomorrow....

—*Matthew* 6:33, 34a

For Gerben and Grace Dykstra, my parents,
Who taught me to trust and to love both by
words and example.

Chapter One

As the deacons took the collection, Joe leaned sideways in his pew, looking past the man in front of him. From this angle he had a better view of the woman sitting in the wing.

Fortunately Joe hadn't seen her until the sermon was over. She might have proved too much of a distraction otherwise.

Her high cheekbones and narrow nose served as an exquisite frame for her almond-shaped blue eyes and delicately curved mouth. He sighed as she lifted a hand to brush her hair from her face, then turned ahead once again.

Joe wasn't a believer in love at first sight, but this woman created a feeling of rightness. He had to talk to her after church.

His neighbor elbowed him lightly, and Joe glanced at Lorna McLure, his old schoolteacher and the wife of his good friend. He smiled at her intrusion.

"You might want to think twice about that one, Joe," she said quietly.

Joe grinned, knowing exactly what she was talking about and unashamed of it. "You know her?"

"Oh, don't turn those puppy dog eyes on me as if I could help you out there." Lorna winked at him. "She's Rebecca Stevenson. Jenna Burke's younger sister."

Joe glanced at the vision named Rebecca. Jenna's sister. This was a major setback.

Jenna Burke was the wife of the local bank manager. She was proud of her husband's position on the town council and their position with the town's elite. But she was even more proud of her family's wealth.

Joe sighed as he watched the vision smile at the deacon as she handed him the collection plate. Without moving an inch, this beautiful woman had suddenly been put out of the reach of a mere truck driver with the dubious last name of Brewer.

"You have enough girls to keep you busy, anyhow," Lorna continued.

"What do you mean?" Joe turned to her, meeting clear green eyes that surveyed him knowingly.

"Kristine James has been spreading it around the café that she has her eyes on you."

"Kristine has her eyes on any single guy who is still breathing," he said with a grin.

"And what about Stephanie and Erika?"

Joe rolled his eyes. "Just where do you hang out when Allister is out on call?"

At that, the tall lanky man sitting beside Lorna McLure leaned over. "And what are you two chattering about?" he whispered with a light frown.

"Jenna's sister," Lorna said with a playful wink at Joe.

Allister shook his head, dismissing the conversation. "Catch me after church, Joe," he said quietly, still leaning forward, his elbows resting on his knees, his hands clasped. "Got a line on someone who is looking for a horse trainer."

As one of the veterinarians in the community, Allister got around and made connections. Joe wondered who he was talking about but knew his good friend would tell him nothing more until after church.

Lorna leaned closer. "And I got a line on Miss Stevenson," she said with a smile. "I hear she's moved here for awhile. I can keep track of her if you want."

"You do that, Lorna," he murmured as he caught another glimpse of Rebecca's eyes. Joe knew he should stop staring, hoping she wouldn't catch him at it. He couldn't help himself. She had a serenity and poise that spoke to a loneliness in his own soul. A loneliness that grew as school friends got married and had children.

He smiled ruefully as the congregation rose for the

final song. He opened the hymnal, letting the music and words pull his thoughts to where they should be.

"Love divine, all loves excelling," he sang. As the words of the song drew him on, he couldn't help but look toward that angelic face once more, a feeling of melancholy pressing down on him.

Someday, he prayed. Someday he would find a love divine on earth.

Rebecca ran her finger over the page of the hymnal as if to absorb the words of the song she was singing, as if to make them alive. She could have sung all three verses of the song without the hymnal, it was so well-known to her.

But knowing the song and experiencing it were two different things. She certainly didn't feel lost in wonder, love and praise as the song promised. Friday she had received a reply on a position she had applied for as a physical education instructor, forwarded to her from Red Deer to Wakely. The message was, "Thanks but no thanks." Her mother had tried to discourage her from applying. "You'll just get disappointed," she had warned.

And Rebecca had been. It seemed no school in Alberta was willing to give a Bachelor of Education graduate who limped a job as a phys ed instructor.

As the congregation closed the books and the minister pronounced the blessing, Rebecca looked at the ceiling of the church. The words of the benediction were as familiar as the song, but they didn't lift her heart the way they once had. As she shifted her weight to her good leg, it was as if she was reminded of her unanswered prayers and struggles of the past months. A year ago she had been offered a position at a high school in Calgary as a physical education teacher. A year ago she had a boyfriend she thought would propose.

The accident changed everything. No one seemed to want her after that.

The organist played the first bars of the postlude, and Rebecca stepped carefully into the aisle, making sure she stayed close to the side in case she held up progress.

"Can you manage?" Jenna came up alongside her, carrying Shannon, her three-year-old daughter.

"I'm fine, Jenna," Rebecca said evenly.

"We can wait until everyone is gone. It will be easier for you to walk out then."

"I'm not that crippled," Rebecca replied, struggling to keep the annoyance out of her voice. She knew Jenna meant well with her overprotective concern. But Rebecca had come to Wakely to get away from smothering love and pitying glances.

"Hello, Jenna." A male voice spoke behind them.

Rebecca could see Jenna's pleased smile and wondered what she was in for now. Jenna made no secret of the fact that she wanted to see her sister replace Kyle.

"Hello, Dale," Jenna said, looking back and stepping aside to make room for him. "Have you met my sister, Rebecca?"

Rebecca politely smiled, turning to face a tall young man. She shook his hand as Jenna introduced them.

"Rebecca, I'd like you to meet Dale Aiken. You'll be working with him at the bank."

"Pleased to meet you," Rebecca said dutifully, looking Dale Aiken over. He was good-looking in a preppy sort of way. Blond hair neatly cut, green eyes and a wide smile that contrasted with his tanned skin. But somehow his good looks and pleasant smile didn't affect her.

"And I you," he said, shaking her hand in a firm grip.

"Dale's father is also one of the bank's chief customers," Jenna said, smiling at Rebecca over Dale's shoulder. "He owns a franchise of hardware stores."

Rebecca didn't know why Jenna thought she needed to know this, but she received the information with a nod.

Dale paused, his eyes on Rebecca. "Are you visiting for awhile?"

"Actually Rebecca is coming to work for Troy," Jenna said. "She's going to stay with us."

"How nice for you to have a sister around."

Jenna agreed and with an approving wink at her sister, walked away, leaving Dale to turn his attention to Rebecca. Rebecca shook her head at her sister's machinations. Obviously Dale passed muster, or Jenna would have hovered until Dale left.

As they walked down the aisle, they exchanged a few pleasantries. By the time they stepped out of church into the bright sunlight, Dale had asked the questions that signal an interest in continuing the acquaintance—where she lived before, what she thought of Wakely, her upcoming job at the bank. Rebecca answered the questions, surprised to find that she didn't mind.

They were chatting at the top of the church stairs when a young woman brushed past Dale.

"Hi, Erika, what's your hurry?" Dale asked.

"Got to catch Joe," Erika replied with a grin. She skipped to the side of another man who began to descend the stairs beside Rebecca and Dale. "Hey, Joe, wait up."

The tall man stopped and looked over his shoulder at the young woman who reached out and clung to his arm. He smiled briefly at her, then his glance moved past her and stopped when he caught Rebecca's eye.

Rebecca didn't know why she held this stranger's gaze. The dimple in his cheek and the sparkle in his brown eyes combined to give him a flirtatious look that should be a warning to any single woman to guard her heart. But her bruised ego needed a lift after the past few months, she reasoned. She'd been mooning over Kyle too long. Having two men show interest in her in one day was reassuring. Emboldened by the attention, she met his gaze with a careful smile.

His expression became serious as he turned toward her. He reached up to finger comb his unruly hair from his handsome face as if in preparation to meet her. Rebecca stopped smiling, suddenly breathless as he took a step nearer.

"How's it going, Joe?" Dale greeted the man with a casual wave, and the mood was broken. Disconcerted at her reaction to the man named Joe, Rebecca looked at her hands, suddenly absorbed in her fingernails.

"Fine, Dale," she heard Joe say. "And with you?"

"Good," Dale replied. "I'll have some news for you in the next few days. I'll call."

"I'll be waiting, that's for sure," Joe replied, his deep voice quiet.

"Joe, don't talk business," Erika said peeved. "Come with me. I want to show you some pictures."

Rebecca couldn't help one more look at Joe. She saw Erika tuck her arm in his. He glanced over her shoulder, his shapely mouth turned up in a grin. He winked at her, and Rebecca felt her heart stir in response.

"That Joe," Dale said with a laugh as Rebecca shook her head to dispel the emotion. "Always got one girl or another following him around."

"You know him?" Rebecca asked, forcing herself

to look away from Erika, envying her slender, perfectly formed legs, the bounce in her step, the man to whose arm she clung.

"We went to school together. In high school, you seldom saw the guy without one or two girls hanging on to him."

Rebecca dismissed her reaction to Joe's good looks. She understood the attraction even as she chided herself for her response. "Doesn't look like much has changed."

Dale shook his head. "I doubt he'll ever settle down." He turned to Rebecca. "But I don't want to talk about him. Why don't we talk about you?"

Rebecca wasn't sure she wanted to discuss that topic, either, but answered his impersonal questions. By the time Rebecca had worked her way cautiously to the bottom of the stairs, Jenna was there to meet them.

"Would you like to come for lunch, Dale?" she asked, smiling at Rebecca.

Rebecca almost groaned and was about to protest.

But Dale accepted gladly, and Jenna flashed Rebecca a triumphant look, which Rebecca chose to ignore. Ever since Kyle had dumped her, Jenna had been pushing her to go out with someone else. And it looked as if she was going to succeed, whether Rebecca liked it or not.

"You're telling me you want the money now?" Lane Brewer, Joe's younger brother, curled his fingers into a fist and glared at his brother. The two sat across from each other at the same scarred wooden table they had used as boys. The air was heavy with resentment.

Nothing had changed, Joe thought, holding his brother's angry gaze. Lane's eyes were hard, his thin lips pressed tightly together.

"Why now?" Lane exclaimed.

"Because I applied for a loan to build my arena and calculated in my share of the ranch as an asset. I need the cash." Joe tipped his chair on two legs in an effort to relax. He tried to stifle the fearful premonition that Lane was going to put him off once again.

"But you told me you could wait awhile."

"When Dad died, I said I could wait until you got things going," Joe replied, rocking lightly in the chair. "But now I have plans. I've applied for the loan. I've gotten a few inquiries from some breeders in Montana to train and show their horses. I need my share of the money to build the arena now. Besides, you have the place up for sale, and you told me you finally have a buyer."

"I can't do it," Lane said flatly.

"What?" Joe let the chair legs fall to the floor with a hollow thunk. "Why not?"

"The buyer backed out, and then I got this." Lane got up, picked a folded piece of paper from the top of a desk overflowing with papers and wordlessly handed it to Joe.

Joe unfolded the letter and skimmed the contents, his heart pounding at what he read. He reread it more slowly, laid the letter on the table and pulled his hand over his face. "When did you get this?"

"A couple of days ago."

Joe leaned his chin on his hand, turning to look out the fly-specked window. The same window he had spent much of his youth looking out, wishing he were anywhere else but here in this old house at this selfsame table. "How did this happen? A bank doesn't begin foreclosure unless as a last resort. How could you let things go so far?" he asked, turning to Lane.

"You said you didn't want to be involved with the day-to-day stuff of the ranch. Told me to make my own decisions. Well, I did. I've had nothing but problems with this place. Disease, a bull that was no good. A couple of lousy hay crops and I had to buy hay. I couldn't keep all the cows we had so I had to cut down. Which made less income."

Lane leaned forward, his gaze intent. "We're going to lose the ranch, Joe. If things go the way the bank is talking, they're going to foreclose. I'll have to declare personal bankruptcy, and I can't do that. They'll run my life for the next five years. I can't stand that."

"I don't know why you say we are going to lose this place, Lane. You got your name on the title when Dad died. All I got was a cash payout." And a small one, at that, which he still didn't have, Joe thought, staring morosely at his brother.

Lane wasn't worried about the ranch, and they both knew it. Lane never did like having people tell him what to do. If he declared personal bankruptcy, he would have someone hanging over his finances for years.

"Joe, this ranch is a part of you." Lane tried another tack.

"Not the best part," retorted Joe. "I'm not exactly awash in fond memories of it." He glanced around the cramped kitchen, its painted wood cupboards still the same grimy cream color they had been all those dreary years that Lane, Joe and their widowed father lived here. Under the table and in front of the kitchen sink, the gray floor tiles were worn away to the wood subfloor. Behind him, the wall sported a hole from Joe's teenage years when he lost his temper over his father's unreasonable demands on his time. He had put his fist through the drywall and kicked a chair across the kitchen. It had no effect on his father. Joe's loss of temper seldom did.

"I don't know where I'm going to come up with enough cash to pay out these loans," Lane continued with a sigh. "The ranch is not selling. I'm stuck. I know you have a bunch stashed away. You gotta help me out."

Joe sighed as he picked up the letter and again read the stilted language, trying to find a way he could salvage something for himself from this fiasco. "Why don't you go to another bank? Get a loan to pay me out?" It was a long shot, and given Lane's financial woes, hardly a solution, but Joe was grasping at anything.

Lane looked at the table, tracing his fingers in one of the gouges as he narrowed his eyes. "I went to the banks from Rocky Mountain House to Okotoks and even to Calgary. None of them would help me out."

Joe put the letter down. "Let me see last year's financial statement."

Lane sighed, pulled at his ear and got up. He riffled through some papers and pulled a large manila envelope from a pile. "Here," he said, throwing the envelope on the table. "I can't make heads or tails of them so I don't know if a high school dropout like you could."

Joe let the slight pass over him as he opened the envelope. Lane would sooner eat glass than ask Joe for help. That Lane had was a measure of how desperate he was. In spite of that, Lane still couldn't stifle his petty tendencies.

A quick look showed Joe that Lane had borrowed on virtually everything he could. The income side of the statement showed a decreasing amount for the past three years.

Joe closed the statement and slid the book across the table to his brother. "I can't help you out. I don't even have a quarter of what you owe in cash, and even if I had less, I wouldn't give you anything. It wouldn't help. You're too far down. You can't sell the place. Live with the consequences and let it go.''

"My brother," Lane said, his voice heavily sarcastic. "This is how a so-called Christian like you helps out his own flesh and blood."

"Giving you money isn't necessarily a Christlike thing. I've got my own plans, Lane."

"Your training arena?" Lane snorted. "Don't be a fool. You don't have enough money without your share of this ranch."

Joe pressed his lips together, praying he could ignore the derision in Lane's voice.

"There's a perfectly good arena on this place," Lane continued. "You could rent it from me."

"We've gone over that already, Lane, and you know the answer. The money from that is only an inch against the mile of debt you have."

Lane slammed his fist against the table. "You haven't changed a bit, have you, you self-righteous—" Lane sputtered, trying to find the right words. "You know what your problem is? You're jealous. You've always been jealous."

As Lane ranted on, Joe reminded himself of the verse in Proverbs. "He who keeps his tongue is wise." He didn't feel very wise right now, because he didn't feel like holding his tongue. And his new-found faith was sorely tested by the grain of truth buried in Lane's many angry words.

Yes, he had been jealous of his brother. Jealous

of the fact that his father's approval was bestowed more quickly on Lane than Joe. That no matter how many blisters and bruises Joe got pitching bales, handling calves or putting in fences, it was never enough.

Joe had struggled with the jealousy Lane accused him of, and it was still a source of discontent in his life that required daily prayer.

Joe held on to his temper, his hands clenched. He took a breath, got up, took his hat off the table and set it on his head. "My advice to you is let the bank take the ranch and then go out and get a real job."

Lane looked contrite as he tried another tack. "I'm sorry, Joe. Really. There's got to be a way to save this place. Doesn't it mean anything to you at all?"

Joe looked around once more. The kitchen counter held dishes from a few meals. The floor was littered with crumbs. Beyond the archway to the living room, Joe saw the couch from his youth covered with magazines. A couple of beer cans lay on the floor beside it. He knew that an inspection of the bedrooms would show him the same things.

It looked much as it had when he was growing up.

"No," Joe said with finality. "It means nothing." He turned and left.

"So after the accident you began your physio program in Calgary?" Heather Anderson picked up a clipboard that held Rebecca's physiotherapy program and flipped through a few of the pages.

"Yes." Rebecca smoothed a wrinkle in her sweatpants, looking around the physio department of Wakely General Hospital. It was smaller than the one in Calgary. But the department in Calgary didn't have Heather Anderson as an employee. And Heather was the therapist Rebecca wanted to work with.

Heather nodded and made a note on the chart. "According to your report, you've sustained some residual nerve damage as a result of the accident. You realize that this can't be repaired no matter who you see?"

Rebecca nodded, suddenly hating the words and what they meant for her life. "So I've been told," she replied, her voice tight.

Heather dropped the chart on the metal table beside the bed in the examining room, crossed her arms and leaned against the wall. "So what makes you think I can do anything for you?" Heather's question was blunt, but Rebecca appreciated her honesty.

"Because I heard you're the best." Rebecca tucked her hair behind her ear and looked up to meet Heather's level gaze. "When I found out that you got married and moved out to Wakely, I knew I had to come here, as well. I read an article about a patient of yours and I asked around. I heard you're hard to work for but I know you get results."

"And what results do you want?"

Rebecca took a breath, hardly daring to voice her faint hope. It hurt to talk about broken dreams and promises to someone who could only help with her broken body. But she knew she had to be honest with Heather. "Before my accident, I just finished getting an education degree with a physical education major. I still have hopes of getting a job in that field someday. For that I need better mobility, and for that I need the help of someone considered the best. I decided to move here to get it."

Heather nodded. "I thought you were going to be working at the bank for your brother-in-law, Troy."

Rebecca wasn't used to having the different parts of her life intersect as they did in this small town. "It's temporary. Troy understands my situation. I sent applications out before I came to work here. I'm waiting to hear back from a few places yet. If something comes up in my field, then I'm free to leave."

"You're fortunate." Heather tilted her head and studied Rebecca from a different viewpoint. "And you're right about one thing. I do expect a lot of work. The first week I figure on having you here every day for an hour and then we'll set up your program. What time can you come in?"

"Troy and I decided I would be working until three. I would like to come in then."

"One thing I want you to be very clear on," Heather said sternly. "What we are doing here is not repair. What we are doing is trying to make your walk look as natural as possible, compensating for the loss by using other muscles.'' Heather raised her eyebrows as if in question. ''I can't guarantee you'll be able to play sports again, or even walk properly, but we can try to get your body working at its maximum capability.''

''I know,'' Rebecca replied, her voice quiet. She resented for a moment the finality in Heather's voice. She looked up, meeting Heather's hazel eyes. ''Miracles are in God's domain, but I intend to do what I can.''

Heather smiled in return. ''Good for you. But we can definitely help, if you're willing to work.''

''That I am,'' Rebecca said emphatically.

''Then we'll see you tomorrow at three.'' Heather picked up the clipboard, shook Rebecca's hand, brushed aside the curtain dividing the examining rooms and left.

Rebecca blew out her breath and slowly got off the bed. She was surprised to see her hands trembling as she changed from her sweatpants to her regular clothes.

It was strange how things had conspired to bring her to Wakely. Heather was known and respected in her field. When Rebecca found out she was working in the same place her sister lived, she decided to make the move.

She mentioned the fact to Jenna, and Troy offered her the temporary job in the bank. She knew this was what she had to do. Working in a bank wasn't her dream, but it was something to do until her leg was stronger.

Rebecca buttoned up her blazer and tugged it straight, making the transition from patient to accounts manager. She caught a glimpse of her face in the mirror on the wall and paused, rearranging her hair. She allowed herself a brief smile. She had a premonition that moving here had been a good decision. Heather would be able to do more for her than the therapist in Calgary, of that Rebecca was convinced.

She allowed herself a moment to dream and to feel that coming to Wakely would change the entire course of her life.

Chapter Two

Joe fidgeted on the upholstered chair and glanced around the bank. Light poured in from an arched skylight, and plants filled corners in an attempt to create an open feeling. He still felt claustrophobic.

The logo on the circular reception desk directly in front of him was a strong reminder of letters and bank statements that his father ignored and that Joe, as a struggling high school student, had tried to figure out. He remembered all too well the clutch of panic when he saw the negative balance on the bank statement, the overdraft charges.

But he had escaped that. He had left the ranch, had worked every waking minute, had scrimped and saved and established his reputation as a horse trainer. After all those years he was finally ready.

A couple of weeks ago he had applied for a loan, and on his way back from Calgary this afternoon,

Dale had raised Joe on his mobile phone. Could he come in as soon as possible? Dale was sketchy on the details, but Joe was pretty sure it had to do with his loan.

Joe leaned his elbows on the knees of his faded denim jeans and ran a hand over his chin. He wished he had had time for a shave and a change of clothes.

Not that he needed to make an impression on Dale, he thought ruefully. Dale had seen him looking worse, but he did want to project a professional image.

He tapped the toes of his boots restlessly against the ceramic tiles of the waiting area, stifling his impatience at the wait. Roy, his boss, wanted him in the city in two hours. He hadn't seen his horses for a couple of days. He was itching to start Talia, his most expensive horse by far. His stake horse. The beginning of an illustrious line, he thought with a wry smile at his dreams.

"Are you sure you don't want any coffee?" Sharla, the receptionist, asked, smiling at him from behind the desk. "It's really no trouble, Joe."

"No. Thanks." He glanced impatiently at his watch. If Dale didn't come in the next few minutes, he would have to get the information over the phone.

He got up and began walking around, trying to stifle his nervousness. His future hung in the balance, and he didn't want to admit it, but he was frightened. Please, Lord, let them approve the loan, he prayed as he paced.

"Mr. Brewer?"

Joe turned at the sound of the quiet female voice, then tried to keep his mouth from falling open. In front of him stood the vision he had seen in church on Sunday, the woman with the angelic face.

"Expensive" was the first word that came to mind as Joe looked her over. Hair, makeup, clothes all had that smooth, clean look. She exuded an elegance that made him feel suddenly gauche and awkward.

"I'm Rebecca Stevenson. Dale is on the phone right now and will join us shortly. I'm going to be sitting in on the interview." She stayed where she was, holding a file folder in front of her, while Joe pulled himself together, suddenly very conscious of his faded denim jacket with the frayed edges and the stain on the knee of his blue jeans.

"Sure," he said, forcing a smile, trying to absorb the information.

"We'll be in here," she said, indicating an empty meeting room with a wave of a well-manicured hand. She turned and walked slowly across the reception area, a hitch to her walk, as if she had hurt her leg.

Joe hurried to open the door to the meeting room, but Miss Stevenson already had her hand on the doorknob. She pulled away at his touch and took a quick step backward. Only she didn't quite make it. For some reason, she lost her balance, one arm flailing, the other still holding the manila folder.

Joe instinctively caught her around the waist, his other hand catching hers. "Sorry about that. You okay?"

"Let go of me," she said through clenched teeth.

Joe obeyed then stood back as she ran a hand over her hair and smoothed down her blazer, then steadied herself, her lips pressed tightly together.

They stood in front of the door for an awkward moment. Then Joe took another chance and reached past her to open it.

"Thank you," she murmured, avoiding his eyes. She walked past him, her movements slow, her limp more obvious.

Joe held onto the door a moment, puzzled at her reaction, then followed her into the room.

Miss Stevenson lowered herself into a chair on one side of a long table across from him. She brushed a hand over her hair, tucking a wayward strand behind her ear, avoiding his gaze.

Joe felt like a heel. "I'm sorry about that," he said quickly, sensing this wasn't the most auspicious introduction. He shrugged, feeling suddenly self-conscious. To cover up, he flashed her a grin. "I thought you were going to fall."

Her hand paused in midair, and her fingers curled against her palm. "I wouldn't have," she answered, her voice chilly.

"Sorry." Joe carefully pulled a chair away from the table. He had obviously stepped over some unknown line. *Just needs room,* he thought. Some of the more skittish colts he worked with were like that. Didn't like being rushed.

Miss Stevenson gave her head a shake, as if to

rearrange her hair, folded her hands on the table in front of her and gave Joe a polite but cool smile. "You can sit down, Mr. Brewer. Dale will be here shortly."

Joe nodded absently. He wondered why she had to be here. Maybe Miss Stevenson would be helping him on the finer details of the loan.

The door opened, and Dale stepped into the room, smiling apologetically. "Sorry about that. Just had to clear up a few things over the phone." He shook Joe's hand, then sat down. "Glad you could come in on such short notice. I take it you and Miss Stevenson have already met?" Dale looked at Joe, then at Miss Stevenson, his gaze lingering on her.

"Yes, we have," Joe said wryly, noticing the way Dale couldn't seem to keep his eyes off Rebecca Stevenson. Not that he blamed the guy. Joe had had the same problem in church on Sunday. But if she was out of his orbit then, her first impression of him put her in another galaxy by now.

"Okay." Dale dragged his gaze away from Rebecca and pulled his chair close to the table. He smoothed his tie as he laid a file folder on the table. "I hope you don't mind if Miss Stevenson sits in on this meeting?" Another coy glance at Rebecca. "She's going to be taking over a few files for me, and I thought this would dovetail nicely into your other plans."

Joe shrugged, feeling like a spectator. A quick glance at Rebecca's face revealed the same composure she had shown in church, the same expression on her face. A real professional, thought Joe, looking at Dale. She didn't seem to mind, or if she did, she didn't show it. "Fine by me," Joe said.

"We're also waiting for your brother, Lane. He was supposed to be here, as well."

Joe wondered what Lane had to do with his loan. But Dale was busy, paging through some papers, and didn't see his questioning glance. Joe didn't want to ask Miss Rebecca Stevenson.

Dale found the paper he seemed to be looking for and pulled it out. He smoothed it on the table and looked up, his expression suddenly serious. "What has happened here is that we were unable to secure financing for your newest venture, at least not in the amount you requested. A couple of factors have come into play. One is the lack of collateral and a dearth of up-front money. Secondly, we don't have enough of a history of that type of business. It's a risky one, from what we can see…"

Dale went on, and Joe felt a clutch of panic gripping his midsection. "Unable to secure financing," were the only words that registered in his numb brain. He forced himself to stay in his chair, forced himself to keep the casual smile curving his lips, forced himself to keep listening as his entire world slowly drifted away from him.

Why, Lord? The words fairly shouted through his mind. Why this? Why now? It was the only thing I ever really wanted. For a frightening moment he saw himself at age sixty, slowly getting out of a truck, his stomach protruding over his belt, his back sore from sitting for hours behind the wheel, eating in some dingy truck stop café far from home. He closed his eyes as if to dispel the image and stifled a beat of anger that Dale had chosen to do this in front of a virtual stranger, and an absolutely gorgeous one, at that. It was humiliating. But Dale was still talking. Joe pulled his mind to what Dale was saying.

"But all of that is moot, considering that you and Lane have made other plans."

Joe's head snapped up at the mention of his brother's name. "Other plans?" he asked, wondering what Dale was talking about. This was the second time he had made puzzling references to Lane.

"Yes." Dale held Joe's baffled gaze, frowning.

Someone knocked discreetly on the door, and Dale, glancing at his watch, got up. "That must be your brother now," he said with a smile. He opened the door, and Lane walked in.

Joe's eyes narrowed as Lane took a seat, ignoring his brother.

"So now that we're here together, we can discuss your other plans, Joe." Dale folded his hands on the file, his cheerful smile encompassing both Joe and Lane. "I'm glad you decided to go this route instead, Joe. I don't need to tell you that your brother's ranch has been floundering for awhile, and you offering to take over his loan would work out better for all of us in the long run." Dale's words finally registered, and

Joe looked at him, forcing to keep his roiling emotions out of his voice.

"What did you say?"

"I'm talking about your offer to take over your brother's ranch." Dale frowned.

"What offer?" Joe leaned forward as if to catch what Dale was saying. He didn't understand.

"I thought Lane talked to you about the trouble he was having with his place. I was under the understanding that you offered to take over the ranch, given the fact that you have a share in the place." Dale raised his eyebrows in a question toward Lane, who shrugged.

"Since when did this come out?" Joe asked, his frustration with his brother reaching critical mass. What could he say without calling his brother a liar in front of witnesses, without making himself look like a fool in front of the calm and collected Miss Stevenson? What had Lane told them to save his own skin?

"Lane approached us yesterday, which, incidentally, was when I got final confirmation on the status of your loan application. He said you were willing to take over the loans."

"Lane was delusional," Joe said flatly, glaring at his brother, who continued to stare straight ahead. "I read the letter you sent him and I saw the financial statement. You can forget it."

Dale looked surprised. "What did you say?"

"If what you said was that you want me to saddle

myself with Lane's debt, then what I said was forget it.'' Joe held Dale's puzzled gaze, ignoring Miss Stevenson and Lane, who was almost squirming in the seat beside him.

''I don't understand,'' Dale said, turning to Lane. ''I understood that you and Joe had spoken. That he had offered to buy out the ranch.''

''When I talked to you the other day, I told you I couldn't pay you the money I owe you, Joe.'' Lane still avoided Joe's eyes. ''You said you needed a place to work with your horses. I thought you meant that you were willing to take it over.''

Joe shook his head, trying to recall what he had said that day, wondering how Lane had fabricated this out of the conversation. Trust Lane to put him in this position, he thought angrily. Joe didn't know what Lane hoped to gain from this, except his freedom at Joe's expense.

Dale leaned forward as if sensing that Joe was weakening. ''You won't be taking on all of the debt. The bank is willing to renegotiate the terms.''

''Maybe you can explain to me how you won't give me money to start up my own arena yet you'd be willing to help me take over a debt that would be almost twice the size.'' Joe pressed his lips together in an effort to stem the tide of angry words inside him. He took a deep breath and covered up by flashing Dale a cocky smile.

''It wouldn't be twice the size, Mr. Brewer.'' The vision across the table from him made herself known.

Her voice was well modulated and quiet, a counterpoint to the anger that Joe held in check.

"Miss Stevenson is right," Dale interjected with a secretive smile at Rebecca. He looked at Joe. "We would be willing to renegotiate the indebtedness."

Joe glanced at Rebecca Stevenson's beautiful perfection and Dale's impeccable suit, both a stark comparison to his faded jeans and scuffed cowboy boots. Suddenly he felt as if he was in junior high school. The ill-dressed, awkward boy being treated with a certain condescending disdain by the rich kids who never had to wonder if their only good pair of blue jeans would hold up, who always had transportation and never had to suffer the ignominy of hitchhiking.

"My name is Joe." It was all he could say. He tilted his head and winked at her. He knew this was not how you treated a banker, but being impudent kept him from being angry. "When you call me Mr. Brewer I feel like my dad."

"I'm sorry. Joe." She refolded her hands, avoiding his gaze. "I've been looking over both your file and your brother's, and I think what Dale is suggesting is not out of the realm of possibility. It would work well for both the bank and yourself. Lane has told us that from a legal standpoint you are entitled to a portion of the ranch. If we foreclose, then try and sell, your portion would be considerably reduced. Therefore, because of your entitlement, your indebtedness would not be as great as your brother's."

Joe looked at her stupidly, then, realizing what she

was saying, shook his head. "Sounds like a pretty good deal for the bank. They would end up with the dumb Brewer, the one who pays back his loans, and he would end up working himself to the bone for you guys." He couldn't keep the sarcasm out of his voice. To have his loan turned down after all his hopes and dreams was almost a mortal blow, and he was having a hard time being reasonable about it.

"You misunderstand me." She looked at him again, her voice controlled, her blue eyes holding the same expression as when they first sat down. "What the bank hopes to do," she explained, "is save themselves the trouble of acquiring real property and then having to dispose of it. There are too many costs associated with that—"

"And it's lousy PR." Joe bristled at her tone, still holding her gaze. He tilted another grin at her, but she wasn't bowled over by his charm.

"There's that, as well," she continued, finally looking away, "but the reality is that the bank is unable to finance a risky venture such as your training facility. The risk to the bank would have been reduced were your brother in a position to satisfy the terms of your father's will. However, we are more than willing to establish a line of credit for you to purchase an established business. You have experience with the operation, and you have some ready cash."

"It always puzzles me that a person needs money in order to borrow money," Joe said, unable to keep the curt note out of his voice.

Rebecca paused. "The nature of the beast, I guess," she replied quietly.

Joe felt churlish. He had snapped and acted like a teenager, but Miss Stevenson had never changed her calm, professional tone.

Of course it wasn't her life that had suddenly been rearranged. It wasn't her dreams that had suddenly died.

Joe had spent half his life watching his father pay off endless interest on overdue accounts and struggle with snowballing loan payments.

And now this cool, contained woman was suggesting he put himself in debt for the rest of his working life on a place he had already slaved on as a youth without payment. It puzzled him how someone with such a serene face could be such a prophet of gloom.

"It sounds like a good deal for you, Joe." Lane finally spoke, then glanced sidelong at Joe. Joe stared back, fighting the urge to throttle his brother.

"Stay out of it, Lane," he replied, his voice devoid of emotion.

"The amount isn't what you think it is, Joe." Dale broke into the conversation and leaned forward to catch Joe's eye. "We are more than willing to negotiate a buyout that would be mutually beneficial to both parties."

Joe held Dale's earnest gaze, wondering why people like him and Miss Stevenson couldn't use ordinary language. "In other words you'll cut me a deal."

Dale shrugged and sat back. "Yes. I guess that's how you could put it."

Dale pulled out another piece of paper and pushed it toward Joe. "Have a look at those figures, and we can sit down and figure out how to make this work the best for the both of us."

Joe nodded and gave the paper a cursory glance. Right now what he wanted more than anything else was to get out of here, away from the eyes of impersonal people, away from his brother, who had put him in this position to start with. He folded the paper and slipped it in the pocket of his jean jacket. "I'll look it over at home and get back to you. I should get going." He got up and tugged on his jean jacket. "I appreciate your advice."

Across the table, Rebecca Stevenson slowly rose from her chair, her expression cool. The only indication she gave that she was puzzled was a faint crease between her arched eyebrows. "It was your brother's suggestion that we were operating under. I'm sorry if we put you in an awkward position. Given that, however, I would just like to reiterate what Mr. Aiken has said. I think this might prove to be a good investment of both your time and money and would be, as I said before, mutually beneficial."

He quirked his mouth in what he hoped was a polite smile. Banker's words. Official and unemotional. "I'm sure it would," he replied, unable to keep the edge out of his voice.

He reached across the table to shake her hand. "Thanks again, Miss Stevenson."

She hesitated, then caught his hand, her clasp surprisingly strong. "I hope I can be of help to you another time, Mr. Brewer."

Not if I can help it, he thought. "Who knows?" he replied vaguely. He turned to his old classmate, forcing himself to remember that Dale had never been deliberately cruel. "Dale. Take care." Dale shook his hand, as well. Joe nodded at his brother, unable to articulate his feelings.

Then he turned, opened the door and escaped.

Chapter Three

Joe strode across the lobby, the sound of his boot heels echoing solidly in the open area. He came to the door, hit the bar with both hands and stepped into sunshine and fresh air.

Dear Lord, he prayed, don't ever make me do that again. That was way too humiliating for a Brewer.

And maybe that's what God wanted, but to be humiliated in front of the beautiful woman he had admired in church and his old schoolmate Dale, who had gone so much further in life already, made it doubly hard.

He took in a lung-expanding breath, and another, as if to clear away what he had just sat through, the demolition of all his hopes and dreams, the depressing thought that he would be sitting behind the wheel of a truck for far too many years yet.

What else does a high-school dropout with only an

instinctive horse sense do for a living, he thought dismally as he lifted his shoulder and reached in his jeans pocket for his truck keys.

"Hey, Joe, you pirate."

Joe looked up to see a slim brunette running across the parking lot, her arms flung out as if to hug him.

"Hey, yourself, Kristine." Joe kept his hands in his pockets, forestalling Kristine's hug.

She stopped in front of him, reaching out to rearrange the collar of his denim jacket. "I didn't know you were in town." She leaned closer, a conspiratorial gleam in her brown eyes. "Are you busy? We could go for coffee."

"Sorry, Kristine. I have to head out to work." He took a step back from her cloying presence. "Maybe some other time."

"Oh, c'mon, Joe." She pouted at him, her full lips gleaming a bright red, her long hair spilling over her shoulders. "What's with you lately? We never see you anymore. I heard you even went to church a couple of times."

Joe nodded, grinning at the expression on her face. "Things change, Kristine. I've changed."

"You must have." Then she shrugged, as if that didn't matter. "But you're as cute as ever." She reached up and rubbed his chin, her hand rasping over his stubble. "Even in whiskers."

Joe smiled what he hoped was a polite but not encouraging smile. "That's a boost to my ego, but I've really got to go."

"Don't be such a stranger, okay?" Kristine tilted her head coquettishly, her hand lingering on his chest.

"We'll see," Joe said vaguely. Then with another half smile, he opened the door of his truck and slipped in. Kristine stepped back as he reversed the truck out of the parking lot, waved and drove away.

Joe blew out his breath and spun the wheel feeling as if he had survived a trial by fire. And ice, he thought, remembering Rebecca Stevenson. It was ironic that the woman he found appealing was out of his reach while the available ones didn't catch his fancy or were totally...unsuitable.

His thoughts shifted to the scene at the bank. He didn't want to think about it. Couldn't. His dreams had disappeared with a stroke of some disembodied pen wielded by a person who had never met him, didn't know him, and only knew his name.

He clenched the steering wheel as he thought once again of Lane's audacity. How had he even thought Joe would go along with his lies?

He hit the outskirts of town, pressed down on the accelerator and tried to outrun his thoughts.

Rebecca drew back from the window and glanced guiltily over her shoulder. But no one stood in the doorway watching her watch Joe Brewer. When she looked out again, Joe was driving his battered pickup away from the bank, and the beautiful young woman who had come running up to him still stood watching him.

A real ladies' man, she thought. Not her type.

Rebecca sat carefully at her desk, forcing herself to forget how easily Joe had caught her when she almost fell in front of him. She still didn't know what had caused her stumble. She hadn't tripped like that in weeks, and of course it would happen in front of a man who, it seemed, had half the female population of this town falling all over him in other ways.

She wrinkled her nose at the memory of his dark hair, dangerous eyes fringed with ridiculously long eyelashes and self-assured grin. Joe reminded her of some clients she had met in her job with the bank in Calgary. Self-assured young men who were cocky until things don't go their way.

Rebecca preferred her men more polished, less overwhelming.

More like…Dale?

Rebecca smiled as she remembered how delighted Jenna had been when Dale had shown interest in her. Jenna made no secret of the fact that she was pleased to see her sister willing to date again. It had been over a year since Kyle and the accident that sunny afternoon.

Rebecca squeezed her eyes shut, fighting off the wave of panic as snatches of unwanted memory returned—her fear and panic as Kyle came after her, the weight of the horse falling on her.

Clenching her teeth, she forced the thought aside. She hadn't had a vivid memory of the accident for months.

Must have been Joe and his reckless good looks. And all that talk about horses.

Rebecca forced her thoughts down other paths, concentrated on her breathing, tried to relax. When her control returned, she slowly turned to her work, picking up the next piece of paper—a copy of a long-term promissory note. She read over the terms, frowning in her attempt to focus on her job.

She only had a few days to familiarize herself with the files in her care. She was determined to show fellow workers that she got this job based on training and experience, not because her brother-in-law was the bank manager.

The phone rang, and Rebecca picked it up.

"Hi, Becks, how's it going?"

"Fine, Jenna." Rebecca grimaced at her sister's use of a name that no one except her family used anymore. "I had my first customer this morning."

"Who?"

Rebecca twisted the cord of the phone around her finger as she glanced out the window again remembering bold eyes and an arrogant grin. "Joe Brewer."

"You must be kidding."

"Why do you say that?"

"Honey." Jenna's voice took on that patient older-sister tone that could still rub Rebecca the wrong way. "You stay away from anyone in this town with the last name of Brewer. They are nothing but trouble." Jenna took another breath, and Rebecca sensed that a unwelcome sisterly lecture was coming on.

"Well, I think I scared him away," Rebecca said, interrupting her. "He could hardly wait to get out of here." Rebecca tapped a pen on her desk as she remembered how quickly Joe Brewer had left. "What can I do for you?"

"I just wanted to see how things are going."

Rebecca resisted the urge to roll her eyes. Dear Jenna meant well, but she was a tad overprotective. "Things are going fine. This is only my second day on the job, after all."

"I know that. I was just thinking about you and thought I would give you a call."

"That's nice." Rebecca closed the file folder in front of her and set it aside. "But I should be getting back to my job, Jen. I've got a stack of work ahead of me and only so much time to do it in."

"You don't have to make a good impression on your boss, Becks."

"Having my brother-in-law as my manager shouldn't make any difference to my work, Jenna," Rebecca reminded her as she tucked the phone under her ear, and reached for a new file.

"I know, but don't forget that you also came here to recuperate." Jenna paused as if to let that sink in.

Rebecca shook her head, wet her finger and flipped open the file. "Look, I've really got to go, Jen. I'll see you tonight."

Jenna said her goodbyes, and Rebecca laid the phone on its cradle wondering if taking on this job in Wakely was a mistake.

But she knew she came here to get help reaching her goal. As she thought of the alternative—living at home with parents who hovered even more than Jenna—she decided she could probably handle her sister.

Joe leaned forward, arms resting on the steering wheel of his semi, his eyes staring sightlessly at the line of tractor-trailer units ahead of him at the weighing station. Not for the first time he winged up a prayer that his load would come underweight, and not over, as he suspected it was.

Tapping his fingers on the steering wheel, he bit his lip in frustration. He had a Super-B full of six-by-six lumber that had to go to a resaw mill in Penticton, and he didn't want to look at his watch to see how late he was.

He pulled out the worn piece of paper that Dale had given him. Each time he thought about the choice between losing his plan to open a training arena or taking over the ranch that held absolutely no good memories for him, he felt almost ill. As he looked at the figure on the paper he remembered all too clearly Miss Rebecca Stevenson's perfectly shaped eyebrow lifting oh so slightly when he refused their generous offer. He was still angry with Lane for maneuvering him into that awkward situation.

Joe folded the paper and set it in the folder on the seat beside him, wondering at the direction of his life.

Trucking was the only thing he knew. He had started driving as an escape, a way to see the world.

Well, he hadn't seen the world, he thought, staring sightlessly at the line of trucks ahead of him, but he'd seen enough of the highways of North America to realize that running from one end of the continent to the other had merely become a job. A way to save for other plans.

Spending lonely evenings hunched over the wheel of his semi, his world narrowed down to the beam of his headlights, then pulling over on an empty stretch of highway to eat truck-stop food and get some sleep was not how he wanted to spend the rest of his life. Lately he yearned for a home, for a certain comfort and routine in his life. The same routine he once scorned.

But what did he have?

Other than his acreage and a small mobile home, his only asset was his innate knowledge of horses. He had gotten started with the help of Allister McLure, one of the local vets.

Allister had fostered and encouraged Joe's gift for working with horses. As an overworked and angry young man, Joe would periodically drop everything and go to the home of Allister and his wife, Lorna. It was Allister who showed him faith in action and Allister who showed him what a father's love should be.

He got Joe started in horse training, recommending

people he met in his practice to take their problem horses to Joe Brewer.

Every few months Joe would purchase a few unbroken one-year-olds from the auction mart and keep them, working with them when he had time and selling them for a decent profit once they were trained. It gave him extra money and established his growing reputation.

He began to dream of starting his own training facility. But until he had his own place, he couldn't afford to quit trucking. And as long as he worked as a truck driver, he didn't have time to expand the business.

He had lost more than he wanted to admit that afternoon in the bank.

He thought once again of Rebecca, allowing himself a moment to appreciate her delicate features, her calm demeanor that both pushed him away and intrigued him. He wished he had been a little more gracious around her. Not that it would have gotten him anywhere, he thought wryly. She was far beyond him. Besides, it looked as if Dale had staked a claim, and he was in a better position to maintain it than Joe was.

A blast from the air horn of an impatient driver behind him made him jump.

Joe put his idling truck into gear and with a chuff of brakes eased his unit forward, closing the gap between him and the truck on the scale. He couldn't resist a quick glance at his watch, which showed him that he was well behind schedule. To get this load to Penticton on time would mean running the risk of a speeding ticket, which he could ill afford. He felt his stomach begin the all-too-familiar tightening as he tried to relax, tried to remind himself that rushing only caused accidents. But he also knew that if he didn't get to the business on time, it would be closed, and he would have to find a spot to lay over, and that meant he would be late for his next pickup in Langley and…

He eased his truck to a halt to wait some more and forced himself not to think about the consequences. Break it down, he reminded himself. First get this truck weighed, then head out, then see what happens. But even as he went through the routine, he couldn't stop his hands from clenching the steering wheel, his shoulders from hunching with tension, something he was doing more and more often.

Taking a deep breath, he dropped his head back. He closed his eyes. "Okay, Lord," he said quietly, "I'm stuck at this weigh scale, and You know I get uptight when I'm behind. But I'm giving You the rest of this day. It's Yours, and I'll live with whatever comes my way." As he quietly continued his prayer, he felt God's peace wash over him.

Slowly his hands lost their grip, and his shoulders fell. He still had to get his load to Penticton on time, he still faced the possibility of an overload charge, but his tension eased. He had reached beyond the tiny confines of his truck and his life, and events were put into perspective.

Half an hour later, Joe was on the road. His load had come in just under. He was still late, but it didn't matter as much as before.

With a quick jab of his finger, he turned on the radio. Immediately songs of heartbreak and sorrow wailed above the engine's whine.

Joe slipped on his sunglasses. One song drifted into another as the pavement rolled along under his wheels, the dotted line clipping by, power poles slowly marking his progress. Joe couldn't help but pull a face as he listened to the lyrics of yet another song about a lonely trucker far away from his family, trying to make a living. Given his current mood, the last thing he needed was to listen to some rich country and western singer making yet another million writing songs about the hard work and low pay Joe was trying to escape.

He hit the power button, cutting off the singer mid-sob, his mind mulling and worrying over his problems.

If he had to shelve his dream of setting up an arena, he still needed to find other work. But trucking and training horses were all he knew. The first gave him a job that earned money, and he had been counting heavily on the latter to help him get away.

He felt as if he was pushed into a corner he had been trying to escape, and he didn't know how to get out.

Chapter Four

~

Joe rubbed his eyes as he leaned against the wall beside the phone at the truck stop, the receiver clamped against his ear. He had driven most of last night and needed sleep more than conversation.

"Hey, Tonya," he said when his renter's wife picked up the phone. "How are things?"

Joe stifled a groan as Tonya began her usual litany of complaints. Her nasal voice in one ear was a sharp counterpoint to the sparse hum of conversation inside the dimly lit café. "I know it's not a palace, Tonya," he said when she was done, "but it's cheap." Too cheap, he often thought. Kevin and Tonya lived there free and in return took care of Joe's horses and boarded their own for nothing.

"Cheap doesn't mean it has to be such a dive," she complained.

Joe clenched his jaw, keeping his temper in check.

Tonya squeezed in one more complaint then Kevin got on the phone.

"Hey, Kevin," Joe said by way of greeting, stifling an urge to yawn. "Just called to see how things are going."

"Well…" Kevin paused. "I… I need to tell you something."

He sounded nervous. Joe knew he had to bide his time. Rushing Kevin only made him stutter.

"It's your new horse, you remember her?"

As if Joe could forget. He had paid more for that two-year-old than he cared to admit to anyone. "Talia."

"That's the one." Kevin sighed, and Joe felt a prickling of fear. "I accidentally put her in the same pen as Mack, and…" He let the sentence trail off.

"And they started fighting." Joe finished the sentence, his throat suddenly dry. Please, Lord, don't let it be too bad, he prayed. I know I paid too much for that horse, but You know why I did.

"Mack is okay, a few nicks and bruises on his chest, but Talia…" Kevin paused again, and Joe clenched his teeth in frustration. "She's, well, she's…"

"Is she dead?" Joe blurted, suddenly frightened.

"No, no."

"But?"

"She tried to jump the fence and ripped open her left flank. It's a bit of a mess."

Joe sagged against the wall in relief, the sounds of

the café drifting away as Kevin's words registered. Talia was hurt, not dead. She's just a horse, he reminded himself.

But even as the thought formed, he knew he was fooling himself. Talia was his stake, the beginning of a larger plan that was supposed to get him away from the wheel of a semi.

"McLure stitched her up," Kevin continued.

Joe felt himself relax. Allister knew as much about horses as Joe did. And Allister would be the next person Joe would call.

Joe ran a hand over his face, weariness engulfing him. The smell of burned coffee had become nauseating. A sure signal that it was time to get some sleep, yet all he wanted to do was run to his truck and head home. "Where did you put her?"

"In the lean-to. McLure gave me some antibiotics that I have to give her with her feed."

"Okay." Joe yawned, his eyes bleary. He had to trust that Kevin would take care of Talia. "I'll be home as soon as I can." Joe placed the phone slowly in the cradle. He still held the receiver, biting his lip, wondering if it was too early to call Allister McLure.

And what would that accomplish? Joe was miles from home. He had to trust that Kevin would do what Allister told him to.

Jenna dropped onto the couch beside Rebecca, blowing out a breath in frustration. "How many drinks do little girls need before they can finally sleep?''

Rebecca glanced at her sister over her book, smiling. "I'm sure we weren't much easier on Mother.''

"We had a nanny,'' Jenna reminded Rebecca, tucking her feet under her. She ran her hand along the rough material of the hunter green couch. "We also had better furniture,'' she murmured, pulling on a loose thread with a frown of displeasure.

"The couch looks fine, Jenna.''

Jenna leveled a patient look at her sister. "You don't need to patronize me. I should have shopped around more when we bought this set, but Troy didn't want to spend that much money. And now look at it.'' Jenna wound the loose thread around her finger and tucked it into the pocket of her jeans. "But there's no way I can justify buying a different suite. Not when I've been hassling Troy about putting on a solarium.''

Jenna was never satisfied, Rebecca thought. The house was only five years old, but she had already added a fireplace to the family room and renovated Shannon and Amanda's bedrooms and the upstairs bathroom. Now she wanted to add a solarium. Jenna didn't want to face the fact that her biggest problem wasn't the house. The problem was it wasn't her parent's house, which was much larger, fancier and more impressive. "This house is plenty big enough, Jenna.''

"I suppose,'' Jenna replied looking around, her lips

pursed. "I'm just used to more. It's very hard to move down the economic food chain." Jenna sighed. "I can't believe you once considered becoming a phys ed instructor. They make even less than a bank manager does. You'd never have been satisfied."

Rebecca said nothing at the unintended slight. Jenna still regarded her as the spoiled baby of the family who got more than Jenna did. "I did more than consider it, Jenna," she said. "I got my degree, and I would have had a job if I hadn't—" Rebecca pressed her lips together. Why was it still so hard to talk about the accident? To even casually mention the loss of her dreams that day.

"Oh, Becks. It must have been hard, I'm sure." Jenna laid her hand on Rebecca's shoulder in sympathy. "I still can't believe Kyle just walked away."

Rebecca could. Kyle felt guilty. He was the one who had lost his temper. He was the one who had gone after her on his horse. When he lost control, he was the one who escaped with only a bruised shoulder. It was Rebecca who had sustained the spinal injury.

Guilt kept him away. She was always thankful that her parents hadn't taken their lawyer's advice and sued. She wanted to put the whole episode behind her. Winning a court settlement wouldn't repair her body. Her parents had more than enough money.

And she didn't want to have to face Kyle and his abandonment.

"I'm sorry I brought it up," Jenna continued.

"You're here now, and I'm glad. Although I don't know why you insist on working. You don't have to, you know."

"Yes, I do, Jenna. I've got that business degree Mom and Dad paid for. I can't pay them back for my education degree, but at least I can do something. I was ready to climb the walls at home with Mother fussing and fretting and hovering over me." Rebecca smiled at her sister, her book forgotten in her lap. "I like the work even if it's not what I always wanted."

"I never could understand why you liked sports as much as you did." Jenna wrinkled her nose in distaste. "And Shannon is just like you. She'll be involved in every sport possible, just like you were. I'm sure we'll need to put in a swimming pool for her someday."

"Honestly, Jenna. Aren't you ever going to be satisfied with this house?"

Jenna withdrew her hand from her sister's shoulder and looked around with a shrug. "I don't know. I'm just wondering what it's going to be like when Shannon and Amanda start having friends over. It seems like we use every square inch of space now. I can't imagine what it will be like then."

"It'll be fine," Rebecca replied. "Do you remember my friend Miriam? They weren't rich, and they didn't have a big house at all, but I loved going to their place."

"Was she that girl who lived on the dairy farm?"

Rebecca nodded, smiling as she remembered

breakfasts around a crowded table and noise and laughter. After breakfast there were chores. It didn't matter who was there—everyone pitched in. "What I remember best of Miriam's place was the space and room outside. Mom and Dad had a huge house in Calgary, but I always felt closed in there. I never felt that way at Miriam's place. I always said that when I grew up, I wanted to live on a place like that."

Jenna punched Rebecca's shoulder lightly. "You're such a romantic, Rebecca. I'm sure you didn't get to see Miriam's parents burning the midnight oil trying to figure out how to make the money stretch to buy enough food and clothes for that brood of kids." Jenna let her hand rest on her sister's shoulder. "You've never had to be on your own, so you don't know how hard it is to scrimp. Take my advice, girl. Marry someone who can keep you in the style to which you are accustomed. Now, more than ever, you have to be choosy about who you marry."

Rebecca bristled at her condescending tone, quite sure she was alluding to Rebecca's limp. It annoyed her that her family saw her as helpless and spoiled. Her sister was no better than her parents in thinking that she would cave if she wasn't dressed in designer outfits or nibbling on gourmet chocolates. Truth was, Rebecca couldn't care less, but no one seemed to get it.

"And how is working with Dale?" Jenna continued.

Rebecca had wondered when Jenna would bring

that up. "He wants to take me out this weekend," she said absently, her eyes skimming over the words to find her place.

"I'll bet he takes you to the Palliser. I loved that hotel," she said wistfully. "Troy and I haven't been there since our third anniversary."

Rebecca had never cared much about where they ate and who they ate with, she thought, noting the faraway look in Jenna's eye. Food was food, she figured. Lobster thermidor or a burger at a fast-food restaurant served the same purpose. They filled you up.

"I'll let you know when he tells me," Rebecca said absently, looking at her book. She couldn't get into the story, but by pretending to read, she forestalled Jenna's other questions. She didn't want to dissect every nuance of Dale's very short phone conversation, nor did she want to talk about what she should wear. Rebecca had more important things on her mind right now. She was still waiting to hear from the high school in Edmonton about her job application for phys ed instructor. She had applied quite soon after her accident, figuring that hard work would get her mobile in spite of what the doctors said. She had the knowledge, and at one time she had the skills. She just lacked the physical prowess. But that would come, she figured. Heather had given her a series of exercises to do that were more challenging. She was enjoying her job, working with people she would see in the grocery store after work or in church on Sunday.

She felt as if she was finally moving in a positive direction.

A date with Dale came somewhere toward the bottom of her list of priorities. She didn't even stop to wonder if that had more to do with her high hopes of pursuing her teaching career—or her tepid feelings about Dale.

Chapter Five

"**S**welling has increased, especially around the stitches." Allister gently touched the leg, and the horse shied away. Joe stroked Talia's nose, holding the halter rope while Kevin hung on the fence of the outdoor pen watching them. "Have you been giving her the antibiotics?" Allister asked.

"Kevin?" Joe asked, looking at his renter. "Have you?"

Kevin chewed his lip as if contemplating the answer. "Well..." He hesitated, looking away from both of them. "She didn't always eat all her feed, and the pills would be on the bottom of the pail. When I tried to feed them to her, she'd let them fall out of her mouth." He scratched his head, still looking away. "You said not to force her, Joe. You said to go easy with her."

"Did you try grinding the pills up?" Dr. McLure straightened, brushing the horse hair from his hands.

Kevin shrugged. "Not always."

"That's why she wasn't eating them." Allister exchanged an exasperated look with Joe, and Joe felt immediately guilty.

Talia threw her head and snorted, and Joe pulled his attention to his horse, holding his rising anger at himself and his renter. Kevin had worked with Joe's horses for the past six months. And in the past two, Joe could see with each trip home that the horses weren't as well taken care of as they should be. He knew Allister could see it, too.

He had let it go too long, but what alternative did he have? Finding renters willing to take care of his horses was difficult. He thought he had neatly solved his problems with Kevin. From the looks of Talia's leg, his solution had created more problems than it had solved.

"I'm gong to give you some more pills," Dr. McLure said to Kevin. "This time make sure you crush them really fine and mix them thoroughly through her grain ration. Make sure you don't give her too much grain, as well," he warned as he stepped back from Talia. He looked at Joe. "I'll have to give her a shot for now. It'll get into her system quicker than the pills."

Joe nodded. He hated giving his horses needles. They were so jumpy afterward. He spoke softly to

Talia as Allister drew up the needle, pulling her head down when he saw Allister ready to inject.

"Hold her easy, she'll jump at this."

Talia barely moved, and that made Joe feel even worse. He laid his head against her neck in sympathy, rubbing her shoulder.

"You can take her back to her stall," Allister said to Joe when he was done.

Joe stroked Talia's nose once more, as if in sympathy. Then, with the gentlest of tugs on her halter rope, he led her slowly out of the pen to the single stall he had made up in the lean-to of his small shed.

He led her in, took off the halter and slid the door shut behind him. Talia whickered, and Joe stopped, looking at her.

"Sorry, girl." He walked back, reaching through the bars of the door, stroking her neck, avoiding her soft brown eyes. "I let you down, didn't I?" he said softly, scratching her behind the ears when she lowered her head for him. "I'm sorry. I'll make it up to you." As he spoke, Joe shook his head. How many times hadn't he heard his father use the same words when a promised trip had been canceled, when his father arbitrarily changed his mind about letting Joe participate in after-school sports and worst of all, when Joe's favorite horses had to be sold to pay bills? Except his father had never been able to make it up to Joe.

Joe patted Talia once more, then left.

Kevin and Dr. McLure were still in the pen, talking. Kevin had his head down and was nodding. Allister was frowning, taking a few moments from stripping off his coveralls to gesture as he spoke. Joe knew from past experience that Allister wasn't bothering to spare Kevin's feelings. When it came to horses, Allister had absolutely no patience for neglect and mistakes.

"An animal can't do a whole lot for himself once he's in a human's care," he heard Allister say, his voice rising as he folded up the coveralls. "They depend totally on us. It's trust, and you just broke it with that filly."

Dr. McLure looked up as Joe came near. "I was just talking to your hired hand." His voice held a note of censure for Joe, as well, and Joe winced. He knew Allister was right, as usual. Talia's injury was as much Joe's responsibility as it was Kevin's. "I've got enough pills in the truck for a couple of days. You'll have to come into the office to get the rest."

"I'll...I'll be in t-town in a couple of d-days," Kevin said, glancing sidelong at Joe.

Kevin was beginning to stutter, a sure sign that he was flustered. Joe didn't feel sorry for him.

"That's okay. I'll go in and get them tomorrow." Joe slipped his hands in the back pockets of his jeans and chewed on his lip as he thought of all he had to get done in the few days he had off from work.

"I'll have them ready for you." Allister nodded and left.

"Just sit tight," Joe said to Kevin. "I want to talk to Dr. McLure. I'll be right back."

Kevin nodded, his head hanging. He reminded Joe of his horses when they had been reprimanded, but he still didn't feel sorry for him.

Joe clambered over the fence, easily catching up to the vet. Allister had one of the boxes of the truck open and was counting pills into an envelope. He licked the envelope shut and handed it to Joe.

"So, what are you going to do about these horses of yours, my boy?" Allister said, leaning against the truck, his arms crossed. Joe recognized his tone. It was one often heard from Allister when Joe had been impatient with a horse he was working with, or too harsh.

Joe poked a hole in the sand with the toe of his old cowboy boots, his thumbs strung in the belt loops of his jeans. "I don't know, Allister. It sure doesn't look like I can keep going like this, does it?"

"I'd say not." Allister squinted against the early morning sun, watching Kevin as he led a bay mare around the ring. "Talia's the most valuable horse you've ever owned, but she's going to lose her value pretty quick if you keep letting amateur cowboys like Kevin take care of her."

Joe knew that. Too well. "I was at the bank the other day about a loan for an arena..." He remembered not only the experience but a pair of cool blue eyes. It bothered him more than it should have.

"And?" Allister prompted.

"They turned it down, and on mistaken information from Lane, offered to help me buy back the home place."

"That could be a solution for you."

Joe found a clump of grass in the sand and began working it loose. "I can't do that, Allister." He looked at his old friend. "I can't go back to that place. You know that better than anybody."

"What's the alternative? More trucking? Giving up on the one thing you love to do? You can train horses on your father's old place as easily as you could on a new place that you started. You'll be in debt, but you would have with your own arena, too." Allister pushed himself away from the truck. "Let me put this all in perspective." He pursed his lips as he counted off on his fingers. "Add up my bill, the medicine and the potential loss of value of Talia. How long do you have to work to make enough extra money to pay for that?" Allister waited for his words to sink in. Joe figured out what the bill alone was going to cost him.

Allister continued. "If all you had done the past two weeks is sit at home on this fence and watch your horses, you would have been further ahead than you are now. You've been driving that rig all over the country and getting by on minimum sleep to make a few bucks that are going to disappear." He laid a hand on Joe's shoulder, smiling at him in encouragement. "I know you're a good truck driver. You're a hard worker. But you're a better horseman. You're also an excellent cattleman and businessman. I know how hard you worked on your dad's place and how little it gave you. But you're not doing a proper job at either of your commitments right now."

Joe crossed his arms and leaned against the truck, chewing his lip as he thought about what Allister said.

"You have to learn not to try so hard on your own, Joe." Allister rolled his coveralls into a ball and threw them in the back of the truck. "You know that God will give you what you need. And you know better than a lot of young men the difference between wants and needs. You're a good horseman, Joe. Think of which job would be a wiser use of the talents God has given you." With that parting comment, he got into his truck and drove off.

Joe pulled in a deep breath and blew it out again, letting his old friend's words settle into his mind.

He closed his eyes, sending out a silent prayer for wisdom and patience. Then he walked to the corral where Kevin stood by the fence, waiting.

"We need to talk," Joe said, leaning against the fence. He let his eyes rove over the fawn-colored hills that flowed to the green of the trees skirting the mountains, reminding himself that these hills had been here long before him and would be here long after. His past was behind him, and the problems he faced were only sandwiched between this particular sunrise and sunset. "You know, Kevin," he continued, "when you first started for me you were doing a real good job, but it seems lately you've been slacking off. What's wrong?"

"It's like this, Joe." Kevin paused, taking a deep breath. "Tonya and I don't think we're getting enough of a deal."

"What do you mean?"

"The horses are a lot of work, and the trailer is pretty small."

"It's big enough for two people, and it's in decent shape. Everything works," Joe said, his voice quiet.

"Tonya doesn't think so." Kevin paused, as if to gather his courage. "And neither do I. I think you can pay us some, besides."

"How much do you think you're worth 'besides'?" Joe clenched his jaw. The nerve of this little twerp. Kevin's neglect had cost him big dollars, and now he dared to ask for more?

Kevin shrugged, fiddling with his belt buckle. "We talked about it and thought that you could put in about three hundred, maybe even four hundred a month. We do a lot with your horses. You're not always around."

"You put a pretty high price on your work, considering the shape Talia's in."

"The horses are more work than you think, and how was I to know she'd be so skittish?"

Joe pushed himself away from the fence, turning to face Kevin. "Okay, let's do the math on this. Your time, feeding and riding the horses comes to seven hours a week. Multiply that times four weeks makes about twenty-eight hours. Say your time is worth twelve dollars an hour. Multiply that out and round it off. That works out to three hundred and fifty a month.'' He paused to let that take effect. ''Pretty reasonable rent considering you get to keep your horses here, as well.''

''So that means you're not going to pay us any more?'' Kevin blinked at him, his watery blue eyes barely visible through his long blond hair.

''No, you little weasel. It means I might start charging you rent for keeping your horses here.'' Joe clenched his jaw and glared at Kevin.

Kevin took a step back, pushing his hair out of his face. ''You can't do that. That wasn't part of the deal.''

''Neither was asking for more money for doing less work. And now I've got a lame horse that is getting worse, thanks to you.'' Joe jabbed a finger at Kevin.

''I d-don't have to t-take this,'' Kevin said feebly, taking another step back. ''I'm going to quit.''

Joe stared at him, his face devoid of expression. ''Perfect.''

''It's not an idle threat. I'll leave.''

''Don't forget your horses.'' Joe stood his ground even as the logical and rational part of his mind was beseeching him to stop. How was he going to take care of his animals when he was on the road? He couldn't quit trucking, he couldn't sell his horses. What was he thinking of?

Kevin blinked as if in disbelief, then turned and strode up the walk to the trailer.

Joe watched him go. As the sound of the slamming door echoed against the buildings, he blew out his breath in disbelief. "Good job, Joe," he said out loud, rubbing the tight muscles at the back of his neck. What had he just done? He turned to the fence, resting his arms on it, staring at the hills. He had just lost his renter. His loan had been turned down. He had a sick horse that needed daily care and no one to do it. His thoughts whirled around his head with no solution.

Finally he laid his head on the fence and his burdens on the Lord.

And as he prayed, he felt his shoulders lose their tension, his fingers uncurl. Slowly, as he let go of his notions of what should happen, God's answer came.

Not in a bolt of lightning, not in a shout from the sky, but in a small voice that waited for all Joe's questions to be spent, all his worries to be released.

Rebecca pulled another paper out of the file folder and glanced at it. It was a copy of a letter from the bank to the Brewer family. In banker's language it informed them that the bank's lawyers advised taking steps toward foreclosure. She set it aside, working her way through a history of missed payments, loan renegotiations and second mortgages.

Rebecca shook her head at the contents of the file. Brewer was not a dependable name, that much she had gathered. The younger brother, Lane Brewer, had written a number of angry letters threatening to take them to court, but nothing had come of it.

"Miss Stevenson?"

"Yes?" Rebecca looked up from her work. Standing in the doorway was Sharla, the receptionist. Rebecca thought she was very pretty, though she wore a lot of makeup.

"Mr. Brewer is here to see you."

At the name, Rebecca's heart gave one hard beat, slowed, then began to race. Irritated at her reaction, she took a steadying breath, glancing almost guiltily at the thick file in front of her, then at the receptionist. She closed the file and pushed it to an empty corner of her desk. "I don't know if I have time. Which Brewer is it?"

"Joe's the one that's here," the young woman answered with a bright smile, her red lips a sharp contrast to her white teeth. Her voice took on the tone that most women her age would reserve for a movie star. "He asked to see Mr. Aiken, but he's gone, so he asked for you."

"Is there an empty meeting room?"

"Yes. Number two."

Rebecca took a steadying breath and picked up the Brewer file folder. "Tell him I'll be right out."

Sharla nodded and left. Rebecca put the file inside her desk. She could have met him here, but preferred the impersonal setting of the meeting room.

She stood up, tucked her hair behind her ear and straightened her blazer. Pressing her lips together, she ran them past each other to smooth her lipstick. For one absurd moment she wondered if she should take the time to put some more on.

Then, rolling her eyes at her vanity, she picked up

an empty pad of paper and pen, stepped out the door and walked down the hall, her soft-soled shoes quiet on the cement floor.

Joe sat in the reception area, hunched over a folder. His eyes looked past it, focused on nothing. His wavy hair was still damp and clung to his head in shining waves, and his square jaw had been freshly shaven. He wore clean jeans this time, and a heavy cotton twill shirt that looked brand-new. He looked masculine and appealing.

When he caught sight of her, he closed the folder and stood up, his dark eyes meeting and holding hers.

Funny that she hadn't noticed before how tall he was, she thought with a sudden twinge of awareness. Nor how his shoulders filled out the crisp shirt.

"Mr. Brewer?" she said quietly, clearing her throat. It suddenly felt constricted with an emotion she couldn't define. "You wanted to see me?"

Joe nodded. "Yes." He tapped the folder against his thigh. "I've come to talk about the loan."

"Okay. Come this way." She turned and walked across the carpeted section of the bank, praying that she wouldn't stumble in front of him.

She held the door open for him. But Joe shook his head.

"My mother raised me better than that," he admonished gently, a smile tugging one corner of his mouth.

Rebecca felt an unexpected flutter in her stomach at the sight of his smile and the hint of a dimple accompanying it. Flustered, she looked away, but paused before stepping through the door.

She walked carefully to the other side of the table. Joe pulled up the chair across from her, waiting until she was seated. As soon as she sat down, Rebecca realized her mistake in choosing this room. The table between them was narrower than her desk. He was directly across from her.

"So what can I do for you today?" Rebecca asked in her most professional banker voice, trying to create some distance. She didn't like the silly, fluttery feelings he created. They made her feel like a goofy teenager.

And like every other woman in this small town.

"I've decided to go ahead and buy out my brother and take over the ranch."

Rebecca's gaze shot up to meet his. "Really? Why? I mean..." She stopped talking before she made a complete fool of herself. After their last meeting, she didn't think he would ever come back. He had been so adamant.

"Things change," Joe said, and leaned forward, his eyes intent on her.

Rebecca took the full force of those deep brown eyes and tried not to sit back.

"God has a sense of humor, it seems," he said with another smile that gave her a strange quiver. "I'm in a situation where I can't help but take my brother up on the offer. Only there are a few things I want to discuss with you and Mr. Aiken yet."

"I see." She clicked her ballpoint and pulled the pad of paper closer. "I've been looking over your brother's file. It's..." She hesitated, biting her lip at her own ineptitude.

"Thick?" offered Joe with a wry grin.

Rebecca's glance grazed his then she smiled in spite of herself. "That it is. From what I read, one of the debts he owes is your portion of the inheritance. As was pointed out before, that would decrease your indebtedness, Mr. Brewer."

"Joe," he said quietly, still looking at her. "I told you before, my name is Joe."

Rebecca acknowledged that with a quick nod, avoiding his gaze. "Okay, then, Joe. What I am going to need yet is information on you. I couldn't find much."

"I have a current financial statement," he said, handing her a folder. "I thought you might need it."

Rebecca took it, and as she looked through it, she gave Joe an apologetic look. "I'm sorry that I haven't had the time to look over your file here. I couldn't find anything, and Dale isn't in today."

"That's because I probably don't have a file." His voice was quiet, and Rebecca looked up to see him smiling at her. His smile wasn't really flirtatious, but his eyes crinkled at the corners and his gaze was direct. The whole effect was flirtatious.

Rebecca held his gaze, then looked away, unwilling to acknowledge his physical attraction. "Why is that?"

"Because I bought what I have by saving for it, not borrowing."

"That's unusual."

Joe shrugged. "I grew up with debt. I refused to get caught in that cycle. I built my place up piece by piece. It took quite a bit of pushing to even apply for the loan."

Rebecca heard the note of pride in his voice and chanced another look at him, but his eyes were averted. He was staring at his hands, a frown creasing his forehead.

"That's quite an accomplishment," she said. And it was. She couldn't imagine the self-discipline it must have taken.

"Not really. It's just a matter of knowing what a person needs and what a person wants." He looked up again, his expression serious. Their eyes held. Rebecca's view of him was rearranged.

"So you're willing to take over the loans as set out in the papers Mr. Aiken gave you the other day?"

"I'd want to do some negotiating on the terms." Joe sat back, folding his hands across his chest. "Especially because it would appear that by taking over my brother's debts, I would be doing you a favor."

"What kind of negotiating?"

"Interest rates for one. For what I'm doing for this bank, I think they can come down a minimum of half a percent."

Rebecca made a note of that. She wasn't sure Troy

would be able to come down much, but it was worth a try. "I'll see what I can do on that."

"So what is the next step?"

"I haven't had a look at the ranch yet. I prefer to make the assessment in person."

Joe shrugged. "Then let's do it Monday at ten and get it over and done with."

Rebecca made a note on her pad. She fiddled with her pen, chancing another glance at Joe. She was agitated to find he was staring directly at her. She forced herself to look away. "Is there anything else I can help you with...Joe?" She couldn't help the hesitation over his name. It created a familiarity that made her uncomfortable.

"Not really. I just happened to be in town...." He let the sentence drift off. Then he set his hands on the arms of the chair in readiness to get up. "I'll see you Monday, then."

Rebecca nodded, but still Joe didn't stand. She watched him for a moment, then realized that he was waiting for her. Feeling suddenly awkward, she quickly stood, swayed as her foot caught in the carpet and steadied herself on the table with her hands. A flush crept up her neck as she faced Joe, who stood across from her, one hand already coming out as if to catch her.

"I'm okay," she said sharply, then was immediately sorry. She wondered what it was about this man that created such a defensiveness.

"I see that," he said dryly, lowering his hand.

Rebecca lifted her chin and tried to hold his gaze as if challenging him. "I'll see you next week then," she said, her voice cool.

He acknowledged her comment with a curt nod. Rebecca looked down, busying herself with her papers as Joe let himself out the door. She berated herself for her lack of control. She never felt this flustered around Dale, but with Joe she was always conscious of her shortcomings.

Chapter Six

Rebecca stood in the foyer of the church and scanned the full pews, clutching her purse. It shouldn't be hard to find a place for only one, she reasoned, but still she hesitated. She knew people would look at her, and that thought held her back.

Early this morning, Jenna and Troy had decided to make an unexpected trip to Calgary to see Troy's family. Rebecca decided to stay in Wakely and go to church alone.

She had considered skipping. But she didn't want to be alone in Jenna's house, and she knew she would feel guilty if she missed. Church didn't mean as much to her now as it once had, but attending was still a part of her life.

But as a result of her dithering at home, Rebecca was late. From the looks of the full seats ahead of her, she would have to make a long walk to the front of the church.

"Trying to figure out where to sit?"

The deep voice made Rebecca whirl in surprise, almost losing her balance in front of Joe Brewer. Again.

And once again, he caught her arm, steadying her. This time, however, she forced herself not to pull away, forced herself to look at him and smile her thanks. She remembered all too well their last meeting. She still felt guilty about the way she had snapped at him.

"Sorry," he said as he slowly released her arm. "I seem to be doing that a lot, don't I?"

"Don't apologize," she said softly, looking down, fiddling nervously with her purse. "I'm the one who should apologize." She chanced another glance at him, feeling even more guilty at the startled look on his face. "I was rude to you the other day at the bank, and you were just being helpful."

"I imagine you get enough people being helpful."

Rebecca was pleasantly surprised at his perception. "You're right," she said quietly, holding his steady gaze. He smiled, and her heart responded.

He stood in front of her, his hand in the pocket of his jeans, holding back a tweed blazer over the same twill shirt he wore the other day. He exuded a rough charm that drew her to him. "Are you alone today?" he asked, glancing around as if looking for her sister and brother-in-law.

"Yes. Jenna and Troy went to Calgary."

Joe was about to speak when an older couple greeted him warmly.

"Good morning Daniel, Elaine," Joe said. He introduced the couple to Rebecca. They said hello, chatted a moment then left. Rebecca felt more than ever that she was a stranger, that she who had so much didn't fit or belong.

While Joe, who owned precious little, did. And for a reason she couldn't quite figure, it bothered her.

"All alone, Joe?" A woman came up behind them, putting her hand familiarly on his shoulder. Her hazel eyes sparkled, and her short blond hair curled around her face.

Rebecca saw Joe raise his eyes heavenward and blow out a sigh. "Hello, Stephanie," he said. He shifted his weight casually, the slight movement bringing him closer to Rebecca. "I'd like you to meet Rebecca."

The woman's bright smile faded, and her warm expression cooled. "Hello," she said, dropping her hand from Joe's shoulder, taking Rebecca's offered one with little enthusiasm.

Joe went through the introductions, and Rebecca almost smiled as he took another step closer to her, as if for protection. At precisely that moment the usher came toward them. "There's a spot for two people in the wing, Joe. Why don't you and Miss Stevenson come with me?"

With a start, Rebecca realized the usher thought

they were together. She was about to protest, but the usher was already walking away. If she didn't follow him it would be embarrassing for everyone.

Joe smiled at Stephanie. "See you around, Steph." He turned to Rebecca. "Shall we?"

Rebecca swallowed as she felt the full effect of his charm. His brown eyes compelled her, and the hint of a dimple beside his mouth made her heartbeat quicken. Without realizing what she was doing, she nodded and turned to follow the usher, Joe right beside her.

She felt immediately conscious of her limp, her slow walk, but Joe strolled easily alongside her, matching his steps to her halting ones. The usher was well ahead of them, and she felt hurried. Rebecca had to concentrate on walking, moving her reluctant left leg, taking a longer step with her good one to make up.

"This isn't rush hour," Joe said quietly beside her, still looking ahead.

Rebecca took a chance and glanced at him. He angled his head, winking at her. Rebecca felt again that curious nudge that his attention gave her and looked away, not replying.

The usher showed them into a seat on the aisle. Joe let Rebecca go in first, and as she settled in he took the order of worship from the usher.

As Joe sat, Rebecca wondered if the usher had figured that Joe was smaller than he looked. It was a snug fit for two.

The people beside them obligingly shuffled aside, giving them a little more room. Joe's shoulder pressed against hers, and she was too conscious of him beside her. She tried to move, but it didn't help.

It was going to be a long church service, she thought, wondering if this was some kind of penance for the sharp way she had spoken to him Friday.

"You have enough room?" Joe asked.

"I'm okay."

"I can move somewhere else if you want."

"No. Don't." It would draw more attention to them. She hadn't imagined the smiles and the knowing smirks Joe got as they walked into church together. She was almost convinced she would be known as Joe's latest.

Joe propped his elbows on his knees as he read through the bulletin. Rebecca tried to look straight ahead, forcing herself not to fidget, to sit perfectly still, conscious of how close Joe was. She envied him his relaxed attitude. Having a woman squashed right up against him was probably normal for him.

Joe glanced at her, his dark eyebrows angling in a frown. "Are you sure you're okay?"

"Yes," she said, a note of exasperation in her voice. "I am fine."

He held her gaze a moment, and it came again, that tingle of awareness, the feeling that she was slowly being pulled into a place she had never been before.

She smiled to herself, though she wasn't quite sure why.

The organist stopped playing the quiet hymns that preluded the service. The minister strode to the front of the church and greeted the congregation, giving Rebecca something more important to concentrate on.

They rose for the first song, Rebecca taking her time getting to her feet. Joe pulled out the hymnal, holding it in one hand, his other in his pants pocket. It was a curiously masculine pose, and in spite of her previous reaction to him, Rebecca suddenly felt good standing beside him. She allowed herself a rare moment of letting someone assist her, having a man holding a hymnal for her in a hand large enough and strong enough to do so without support.

With a rueful smile at her reaction to him, she pushed thoughts of attraction and unsuitability aside and concentrated on the song.

"God is our refuge and our strength, our ever present aid." Rebecca sang the familiar words of Psalm Forty-six by rote, hardly needing the book to follow along. She heard Joe's voice ring out in an even baritone beside her, saw one toe of his cowboy boot tapping lightly in time to the music. He was smiling.

She glanced at the words, suddenly ashamed of how easily the song tripped off her tongue. It could have been a nursery rhyme, for all the attention she had paid to it.

They were on the last verse. "Be still and know that I am God, the Lord whom all must claim."

Rebecca felt her voice falter as she thought of the

battles she had been fighting the past year. Being still had not been her way.

"The God of Jacob is for us a refuge strong and sure." Rebecca swallowed a knot of pain. Refuge. She yearned for it, and for the peace the word promised.

But she didn't know if she could give up the battle to get it.

Then the song was over. Joe closed the hymnal and waited until Rebecca was settled before he carefully sat beside her.

She had a little more room than before and was grateful for that. However, as the service went on, Joe began to get restless. Finally he sat back, one arm resting along the pew behind her.

Rebecca sat perfectly still as she felt the light brush of his arm against her back. She was completely aware of his hand dangling inches from her shoulder, the warmth of his arm along her back and his body beside hers. She felt surrounded by him. Refuge, she thought with a peculiar catch in her throat.

For a brief moment she let herself indulge in a fantasy. She belonged to this darkly handsome man with the compelling eyes and heart-stopping smile. His arm around her protected her.

He glanced at her, and as their eyes met, it was as if an unseen force kept them connected, kept their eyes on each other.

Rebecca felt her breath slow and all else around

them become as nothing. Then, with a shake of her head, she looked away.

She forced her mind to the service, listening to the minister as he finished reading the Bible passage from Job, chapter twenty-two. "Surely then you will find delight in the Almighty and will lift up your face to God. You will pray to Him, and He will hear you, and you will fulfill your vows. What you decide on will be done, and light will shine on your ways."

The minister laid the Bible down and began his sermon. She struggled with what he was saying, that God is intimately connected with us, that He hears our prayers. He talked of Job and his trials.

Rebecca tried to let his message become a part of her, but it didn't gel. Job had many trials, but she knew how the story ended. His wealth and health were restored. He had more children.

Rebecca had been told quite clearly the end to her story. She would never walk properly again in spite of her many fervent prayers. Just a few minutes ago she had been reminded of it when she stumbled. How often had she begged, pleaded for the memories of the accident to be eased, for healing and wholeness so she could do the job she had been working toward since she was fourteen.

Her parents kept telling her to trust, to lay it all in God's hands and leave it. But this was something Rebecca didn't do easily, and she knew it better than anyone.

Rebecca looked at her leg, at the expensive pantsuit

that disguised but could not totally hide her disability. A disability that her ex-boyfriend, Kyle, couldn't see past.

Joe stretched out his legs, and Rebecca couldn't help but give him another sidelong glance. He leaned forward, concentrating, a light frown drawing his dark eyebrows together. He moved his head, caught her looking at him, flashed her a quick smile, then turned his attention to the minister.

Rebecca faced forward. Caught staring like some foolish teenager. She could feel her cheeks heating as she berated herself. She was no better than most of the women in this town.

The service was almost over. When they rose for the final song, she paid attention to the words, ashamed of her lapse. She was here to worship God.

She kept her eyes glued to the hymnal, her face turned toward the front of the church as the minister pronounced a blessing. But try as she might she couldn't help but notice Joe's hands resting lightly on the pew in front of him, his head bent and eyes closed as the words of benediction rolled over them all. And for a brief moment she envied him his obvious devotion.

A devotion that had been missing from her life for awhile.

Joe stayed at Rebecca's side as they walked out of church. He didn't want to break the contact that sitting together in church had given them.

He had seen her pained expression as she looked intently at the words of the hymn. He caught a puzzled look from her after a prayer. He sensed that all was not right in her relationship to God, and he sensed that it bothered her. She intrigued him.

"Is your sister going to be back when you come home?" Joe asked, wanting to break the bubble of silence that surrounded them amongst the chatter of the exiting congregation.

"No. She's going to be gone all day." Rebecca's reply was quiet.

Joe nodded, racking his brain for something else to say. He didn't want to leave, yet felt foolish walking alongside her saying nothing.

"You still figuring on coming tomorrow?" he asked as they made their way through the foyer.

"Yes."

"Do you know how to get to my place?"

"No. You'll have to give me directions." She paused, then finally looked at him. "Good thing you reminded me. I have some paper and pen in my vehicle. Maybe you could draw me a map?"

"Sure." Joe grinned.

They walked to her vehicle, and as Rebecca unlocked it, Joe admired its sculpted lines. A pricey sports utility, that much he knew.

"I imagine this machine is handy for running around the country," Joe commented.

"I like the four-wheel drive," she said. She got into her seat and reached inside the glove box, then pulled out a pen and an old envelope. "That's all I have, I'm afraid," she said with a quiet laugh.

Joe smiled at her, set the envelope on the hood of the truck and quickly sketched directions. "Just make sure you take the second left out of town, and it shouldn't be too hard to find."

Rebecca nodded and glanced at the paper as she took it from him. "Thanks," she said. With another careful smile, she closed the door.

Joe watched as she put on her seat belt and bent over to start the engine. But nothing happened. Frowning, she tried again.

She opened the door. "Do you know anything about cars?"

Joe laughed. "I'm supposed to, but I'm afraid I don't. The best I can do is offer to frown at the engine."

Rebecca laughed. "You're a truck driver and you don't know everything there is about trucks?"

"I know enough about diesel engines to get me by, but this is a whole other system. Pop the hood, and I'll have a look."

And look was all he did. Joe sighed when he saw the sheer mass of the engine, belts and parts tight against each other. Economy vehicles, he thought with disgust. It took a mechanic just to change a fan belt on one of these things.

"Did you find out what was wrong?" Rebecca called.

"Yah. It won't start," he said with a laugh. "I'll

get my truck and we can try to boost it. Maybe the battery is dead."

Joe turned, jogged across the quickly emptying parking lot to his truck, started it and brought it over. He popped the hood of the truck and couldn't help but see the contrast between her still-shiny undented truck and his slightly rusted one.

But the battery wasn't dead, neither was her vehicle out of gas. "Well, that's emptied out my storehouse of information," said Joe as he closed the hood of his truck. "Why don't you leave it here and I'll give you a ride," he offered, taking note of her pale pantsuit. He hoped his front seat was clean enough.

"Okay," she agreed slowly. "You don't mind? It's a bit out of your way, from the looks of your map."

"I wouldn't offer if I minded."

"Okay. Thanks, then." She pulled the keys out of the ignition and closed the door. Joe hurried to the passenger side of his truck and opened it.

He didn't know if he should offer to help her get in or stand back and watch, but she managed. Joe closed the door behind her.

The drive to Rebecca's sister's house was quiet. Joe figured he had used up all his conversation on the way out of church. He didn't mind. Sometimes being quiet together was a good way to get to know someone.

The land flowed past, the dull roar of the truck the only sound. Joe glanced at Rebecca occasionally and was disconcerted to see her looking at him.

He wondered why a glance from her could make him feel so flustered. That hadn't happened since junior high school, when he promised himself to never let anyone make him feel inferior or insecure again.

"Turn here," Rebecca directed, when they were out of town.

Joe recognized the subdivision. The Golden Ring, it was referred to around town, or Snob Hill. He didn't think bank managers made enough to live here.

Troy had done something right, he thought as he turned into the driveway Rebecca pointed out. The gray stucco house wasn't quite as large as some of the others they had driven past, but it was still impressive.

"Nice place," he commented as he drove up the half-circle drive and came to a halt by the front door with its portico and pillared entrance.

"Jenna thinks it's too small," said Rebecca with a laugh as she turned to Joe.

"She should see my trailer." Joe bent to get a better look at the house. It was two stories, the pillars reaching up to the second floor. On one side of the entrance was a bank of three garage doors. On the other a huge window topped with a half circle was covered with its own peak. The roofline was a dizzying combination of dormers and recessed windows. "This house looks…not cheap," he said.

Rebecca laughed. "It's still just a house. You want to come inside for a cup of coffee? It's the least I can do for the drive home."

"I don't know." Joe looked at his feet and took refuge in humor. "Have cowboy boots ever entered those hallowed halls?"

Rebecca laughed again. "There's always a first, Joe."

"Okay," he said with a shrug. "I might get some neat renovation ideas for my trailer. Or, better yet, my old house."

Space was the first word that came to Joe's mind as he slowly followed Rebecca inside, feeling like a rubbernecking tourist. He couldn't help it. He had never seen a house with ceilings this high. The sound of his boots on the tiled front entrance echoed hollowly in the vast emptiness that soared above the living area to his left.

"Does this place have one of those 'you are here' maps?" Joe said, slipping his hands in his back pockets, rocking on his heels.

"It's not that big," Rebecca said, smiling. She walked down a wide hallway, then turned right.

"I'd hate to see what you think of as big, then," he said as he followed her, giving the living room one more look over his shoulder.

"My parents' house is big. Big and empty." Rebecca dropped her purse on one of the gleaming marble countertops and with the ease of familiarity pulled out a coffeepot and filled it with water. "Do you like flavored coffee, or shall I make you an espresso?"

Joe frowned at her. "Can I have just plain old coffee?" he asked.

"I'm sure we've got some of that around."

Joe stood awkwardly in the doorway looking at the small but functional kitchen. "For as big as the rest of the house is, this room isn't very large."

"I know. It's kind of silly, actually. I had a friend who lived in the country. Her parents had this huge kitchen, and everything happened there." Rebecca flicked the switch to the coffeepot and pulled mugs from a cupboard. "They did homework on the table, played games, ate, read the paper. It was great. Like a family gathering place." She leaned her elbows on the counter, tilting her chin at the white table with its stark blue cloth. "That table barely holds the five of us. The formal dining room is much larger, but it's only used to entertain."

Joe wandered across the shiny white tile floor to the bay window by the table. It looked out over a deck on which sat white wicker furniture. The deck was built in several levels, accented with overflowing pots of plants. The yard was a large expanse of green edged with shrubs and flower gardens and surrounded by a high white fence. A few toys were strewn across the grass, and there was a swing set in one corner. "Do they have neighbors on each side?"

"And across the back," Rebecca added, walking to the window. "Jenna wants to put a solarium and swimming pool outside this door."

"Wow."

"I guess." Rebecca shrugged as she walked around the counter. "Do you take cream or sugar?"

"Nothing, thanks."

"Ah. A real man's drink." She poured coffee and brought the mugs to the table. "Do you want to sit in here or outside?"

"Outside, if you don't mind. It's too nice to be in."

"We'll have to go through the garden doors in the family room." Rebecca led the way through an arched doorway framed with carved wood, painted white, to another large room. Joe caught a quick glimpse of leather furniture and hardwood floors, then Rebecca was opening the French doors to the deck.

Joe shook his head as they settled into the wicker furniture. "How many rooms does this house have?"

"I haven't counted." Rebecca sipped coffee and glanced around the yard. "The house is nice and the neighborhood is nice, all these acreages, but I still feel closed in here. In Calgary my parents lived on a hill, but there were houses all around us. If I snuck into my parents' bedroom, I could just catch a glimpse of the mountains. I had to ignore all the other houses, though." She sat back with a sigh. "I would love to live in a house with an uninterrupted view of the mountains."

She would love my place, thought Joe with a rueful grin. "So what are you going to do about your vehicle? Did you want me to phone someone?"

Rebecca shrugged and brushed her hair out of her face with an elegant gesture. "Who do I call?"

"I can give Wierenga's garage a call. They'll come

out and have a look first thing in the morning. He prefers not to work on Sunday, but if you really need it, he can look at it today.''

''It can wait until tomorrow.'' She turned to him with a soft smile. ''If I don't show up tomorrow, you'll know why.''

Joe took a quick sip of coffee. He felt out of place sitting on the deck of this expensive house, yet he was loath to leave. He didn't want to go back to his empty trailer. He didn't want to leave Rebecca. ''What got you into banking?'' he asked, taking a tentative first step to knowing this beautiful woman better.

''A promise I made to my parents.'' Rebecca pushed her shoes off and pulled her good leg up, wrapping her arm around it. ''I took a business course as part of a deal to let me take my physical education major.''

Joe almost dropped his coffee cup. He looked at Rebecca again. Same slender figure, delicate features, expensive-looking clothes. He couldn't imagine her taking something as ordinary as a physical education degree.

''You look surprised, Joe,'' she said with a forced laugh, pleating the material of her pants. ''I didn't always have this limp.'' She stopped, her fingers clenching.

''Sorry. That's not why I was surprised. Truly.''

''Then why?''

He could hear the tension in her voice, knew that she didn't believe him.

"Well," he said carefully, keeping his eyes on the dark liquid in the bottom of his cup, "I just can't imagine you doing something as inelegant as chasing a basketball and sweating."

She laughed lightly. "Thanks, Joe," she said, her voice quiet.

Joe chanced a look at her. She was smiling, and his breath caught as their eyes met. He felt an undeniable urge to maintain the contact, a surprising need to connect with her.

He nodded, then looked away. He was crazy to even entertain any thoughts of attraction to this woman. She was so out of his league, it was pathetic.

Joe took a last sip, feeling suddenly restless. "Well, thanks for the coffee," he said slowly.

Did he imagine the disappointment in her face? Or was it just wishful thinking?

"Sure," she replied. "I'll see you tomorrow. If I can get that truck started." She got up, but Joe put his hand out to forestall her.

"I'll find my own way out."

"Okay. Yell if you get lost."

Joe stood, grinned at her and couldn't stop a playful wink as he turned. He found his way out and drove away, taking another look at the house in his rearview mirror.

Rebecca had said it wasn't as big as her parents' house. He wondered what that place looked like. Then he decided he didn't want to know.

Chapter Seven

꙳

Joe stepped onto the deck of his trailer, his eyes following the contours of the land, his ears appreciating the echoes of the blackbirds. The sounds fed his soul.

Last Monday his life was headed in one direction. This Monday he contemplated taking over his brother's ranch.

And in a few hours he would see Rebecca again. Joe smiled a lazy smile as a picture of Rebecca came to his mind. Last week she had been a beautiful dream. And now…

Joe gave his head a shake. The small trailer behind him was a potent reminder of what he had, and Jenna's house was a reminder of where Rebecca came from.

He knew money didn't buy happiness. He often thought of what the Psalmist said. *Give me neither riches nor poverty.* He had the poverty and knew from personal experience how hard it could be to serve God lovingly when there wasn't enough to eat and when he was teased about patched and worn clothes. His lessons in humility hadn't caused him any lasting harm, but he didn't wish on anyone the money woes he had grown up with.

So why was he on the verge of taking over the very place where he had felt those woes?

He felt a clutch of panic as he thought of the debt, the struggles that would come along with it.

Delight yourself in the Lord, and He will give you the desires of your heart. Joe let the words settle his rising fear.

He took a steadying breath, appreciating the fact that he was outside, standing on the step of his own home. It was a beautiful spring day, and he wasn't driving down an endless road, wishing he were anywhere but in the cab of a semi. The blackbirds were warbling and swooping through the trees behind him. He caught sight of an eagle soaring on an updraft, wings spread. He drew in a huge breath, feeling the space surrounding him. Thank you, Lord. Whatever happens, this feels like the right decision.

Joe smiled as he walked to the horse paddock, the brown spring grass dry under his feet. The morning's chill had been warmed by the sun.

Talia was in her pen, watching him as he approached. She had settled down in the past few days.

"You're doing great, girl," he said, standing by her a moment, not reaching out.

Talia looked at him as if puzzled. Then Joe clucked a welcome, and she put her head over the fence. "Good girl," he said, stroking her head. He climbed over the fence rather than use the gate he had painstakingly put in on Saturday.

Joe absently scratched her head as he looked over the empty land. His brother's place was just over the next rise, and beyond that was leased land. He was going to ride over and check out the pasture, the fence lines and the cows.

And, he hoped, meet Miss Stevenson.

Talia pulled away. Joe watched her as she threw her head and snorted, jogging around the pen and stopping.

"You have your fun now, girl," Joe said with a smile. "You're going to the round pen in a couple of days." The round pen was where Joe started his horses and joined with them, the first and critical step in the training process with any horse no matter what its history.

Joe caught Mack and got him brushed, saddled and bridled. He gathered the reins and mounted. Mack stood quiet, ready to find out what Joe wanted. With a cluck and a shifting of his weight, Joe let him know.

The sun shone warm and soft. It was the kind of early spring day that held a feeling of promise and expectation. The land beckoned. Turning his horse toward the hills, Joe headed into the fresh morning.

Lane's place was just over the hill. As Joe crested it, he pulled Mack in. With a creak of saddle leather, he leaned forward, his eyes traveling over the corrals, the barn and the large structure Joe and his father had built years ago.

The arena wasn't large. He looked past the peeling paint and the missing tin from the roof and thought the structure would be workable for a couple of years.

He remembered late evenings after his chores were done, training horses, practicing the lessons Allister taught him, learning to communicate with the horses, understand them. It was his only truly happy memory, he thought.

A figure strode across the yard toward the corrals. Joe toed Mack lightly in the ribs, and he moved down the hill toward Lane.

Lane stopped as Joe approached and dismounted.

"Hi," Lane said simply as Joe tied Mack to a hitching post. Lane hunched his shoulders, shoving his hands in his pockets. "So, have you decided what you're going to do about this place?" he asked, coming directly to the point.

Joe caught his brother's worried gaze. "I thought I would have a look over the yard, for starters. You can show me what needs to be done, and I can figure out how much I'll have to borrow to get things going. I'm supposed to meet Miss Stevenson here in a few hours."

"Is that the gal at the bank?"

Gal. Joe supposed the word was slightly better than dame, but it was hard to see the immaculately groomed Rebecca Stevenson as a gal. "Yes, it is," he said.

"Have you taken her out yet?"

Joe ignored the comment.

"Haven't, eh? You losing your touch, Joe?" Lane scratched his head, grinning.

Still Joe said nothing.

"Okay, then. Be that way. I've got a late cow calving in the back calving barn. We can start with her," Lane said, pulling open a wooden gate.

Joe took note of the loose hinge. As they walked through the warren of holding pens, his practiced eye saw more repairs that needed to be done. Boards hung loose or were completely gone. The loading ramp had huge gaps where lumber was missing. The cattle squeeze bowed out from the pressure of too many bodies forced into its confines.

He tried not to get downhearted as he paused to grab a large post. He gave it a tug, relieved to feel that it was solid, as was the next one.

"I've got the cow in the far end of the barn," Lane said as they climbed over the last fence. "I think she's working on two."

The cow lay on her side on a pile of dirty straw, her head extended. Joe walked carefully to her to check the name on her ear tag. "Pudge" he read with a start of recognition. He looked at Lane. "Is this that heifer that I bought from Allan Derks?"

Lane nodded, his hands in his pockets. "She's been pushing all morning, but nothing's happened."

Joe kept his mouth shut as he walked slowly around the cow. He couldn't help but smile, though, as he saw one tiny hoof poking out the back.

Joe crouched in the dirty straw trying to grasp the soft, wet leg of the calf. The cow pushed again, and the legs moved.

"C'mon, girl," Joe encouraged, "you can do this." He gave another tug as the cow pushed.

A few more pushes and the first calf slipped out. The cow raised her head as if to say, "Do I have to do this again?" then laid it down again. The hooves came out with the first push, then the knobby knees, the head. A few more pushes, and it was completely out.

Joe quickly wiped their mouths free of mucus, a sense of wonder building in him.

Two small, wet bodies lay at his feet, their legs already working as they tried to get up. The cow heaved to her feet and wavered a moment. Then, without giving Joe a second glance, she turned and began licking her calves. Her tongue rasped over them as their heads bobbed and wove. They were already looking for their first meal.

Joe hunkered down, smiling at the miraculous sight. It's always such a miracle, Lord. Thank You that they're both alive.

How many calves had he seen born, he wondered as he watched the small creatures. How many had he helped along? He had sat watch over cows with a flashlight in biting cold evenings, had watched in wonder on a warm spring day.

The sun warmed his bare back and caked the blood on his arm. He didn't care. Watching the cow he had purchased as a heifer, he felt as if he had come full circle.

He had tried to get as far away from this place as he could. Now he stood in a place he had many times before, grinning like a kid over the sight of two baby calves stumbling around.

Joe got up slowly, wiping his hands with a precious bit of clean straw. He hoped he had time to wash up before Rebecca came.

As he slipped his shirt on, he was unable to look away from the miracle of birth and life. Two perfectly formed creatures, nothing missing, absolutely complete, had come into this world. In a few hours they would be dry, the patches on their forehead a gleaming white contrast to the soft brown of the rest of them, their tummies full.

"What? Out already?" Lane came up behind Joe, holding a rope.

Joe nodded, smiling at the sight. "Yeah. Isn't it incredible?"

"Incredible they lived." Lane shrugged. "Well, that's done. Did you want to see the rest of the herd?"

Joe watched the calves, stumbling weakly around looking for something to eat. It never ceased to amaze him how quickly they were on their feet. "I'd like to wait to see if they drink."

"They'll be okay. The worst part is over." Lane lifted his hand, glancing obviously at his watch. "I've got to get going. I've got a job interview with Jaydee contractors."

Joe looked once more at the calves, then at his brother, and made a sudden decision. "Why don't you go to your interview. I'll look around on my own."

"Well…" Lane hesitated. "I'd just as soon show you around myself."

"I can probably find my way around," Joe said, striving to keep his voice even. "I've spent enough time here."

Lane glowered at him. "I've made a few changes since you worked here, you know," he said defensively.

Joe didn't bother replying to that.

"I've been busy, too," Lane continued.

"I'm sure you have."

Still Lane hesitated. "The cows with calves are in the first upper pasture. The heifers are in the second," he said. Then he turned abruptly and left.

Joe took a deep breath and blew it out. He knew he would find more on his own than he would if Lane came. And he suspected Lane knew that.

One of the calves had finally latched onto their mother's bag and was sucking noisily. The other was still nosing around her front end, as if uncertain where to go. The cow lowered her head and nudged the calf toward her back end. It wobbled on its feet and turned.

Joe laughed, watching them, remembering countless other calvings he had witnessed. It was always with the same sense of wonder he had just experienced. There had been good times here, he conceded.

Joe took the long way back, going over fences, checking out gates as he went. He would have his work cut out for him if he took this over.

Mack was waiting patiently for him, but Joe took a moment to run to the house to wash up. He tried to ignore the towels on the bathroom floor, the stains on the worn countertop, the fly-specked mirror. From the looks of it, he would be further ahead if he torched the house and moved his trailer on the yard. But that was a decision for another time.

Joe stepped into the warm spring day and walked to his patient horse. He climbed slowly in the saddle, looking around as he did so. The mountains were still there, the sky was still blue, and the wonder of the morning easily brought back the peace he had. A sense of rightness pervaded him as he rode through the hayfield. By the time he got to the cows, his spirits had lifted, and his heart was raised in prayer.

Who knows, he thought as he watched calves running through the pasture, kicking their heels. Who knows what could come of this?

Rebecca kept one hand on the wheel, quickly glancing at the map in her hand. "One more turn," she said to herself. She had plenty of time, but she didn't want to get lost.

Rebecca laid the map down, sighing as she turned onto the road indicated. She was glad to get away from the bank. Glad to be driving in the country. It gave her space to think, to sort out conflicting emotions.

She had moved to Wakely to get away from her mother and ended up living with her sister. She held a temporary job while she waited for news on her application at a high school in Edmonton. Heather was encouraging, but she held out no promise of any major improvements in mobility.

Rebecca pulled a face as she slowed down. She was afraid to think what she would do if that application came back. She tried to be positive, but she still had to be realistic. She had to learn to make short-term goals. Get more mobile, get rid of her limp. Long-term dreams were only an amalgamation of short-term ones.

The road curved, and once again the land spread out before her, hills rolling away to mountains. Thankful for the diversion, she watched them, bemused at their beauty and grandeur. How many times are mountains mentioned in the Bible, she wondered. On a trip to Israel she had seen the hills of Israel and often wondered what the Psalmist would have said had he seen these boundless ridges and peaks.

Finally she stopped her vehicle, turned off the engine and got out. Disregarding the dust that filmed the truck, she leaned against the hood. She allowed herself to enjoy the curves of the land rolling up from the plains behind her to the soft brown hills ahead of her. Beyond them, silent and watchful, stood the rugged peaks of the Rocky Mountains softened by distance.

A breeze as gentle as a sigh lifted her hair from her bare neck and teased along her arms. A cloud sifted across the sun, cooling the air. She watched its shadow move along the hills, wishing for the peace that permeated the far hills to come into her life.

She had been going to physio every day for the past week. She was working harder than she had ever worked. Instead of progressing, Rebecca felt her limitations more than ever. She wondered again what she hoped to accomplish, what her real purpose was.

Rebecca looked at the mountains once again, as if waiting for an answer. Only the faint rustling of the wind in the trees drifted to her.

For a moment she indulged in a fantasy, pretending that she was undamaged once again, that she could run across the road through these hills, that she could climb the rugged peaks in the distance.

A twinge in her leg was a potent reminder of reality. She was a cripple who lived with her sister. Sooner or later she would move to a larger bank in the city, a larger office and more files.

And then what?

Rebecca clutched her arms just a little harder, unwilling to think that far. She had spent enough time in the past year dwelling on what she had lost. She knew she had to move on. The trouble was, right now she didn't know where she was headed. She didn't mind the work she was doing. It just wasn't her dream. At least it was better than the impersonal work she had done in the bank in the city. Now she had a chance to build some kind of rapport with clients.

Clients like Joe.

Rebecca's heart couldn't help but quicken as she thought of meeting Joe again. She got into her vehicle and drove on.

The road curved into a small valley cut by a creek and edged with aspen trees. She rattled over a bridge and came upon a driveway. A sign hung from a post beside the road proclaiming it to be The Brewers. Rebecca slowed, then drove onto the yard, swallowing her trepidation.

The driveway veered to the right, curving around a small house. To the left Rebecca could see some fences and a building that looked like a large barn with sliding doors on the end.

The heavy wooden doors hung at a crazy angle, and Rebecca could see piles of lumber in what looked like an alleyway. Must be the old arena mentioned in the real estate report.

No vehicles were parked by the house, and for a disappointing moment Rebecca thought Joe had forgotten the meeting. She looked around, holding the steering wheel, deciding what to do. Maybe he was in the house.

She got out of the car, taking a moment to look around the yard. It was well sheltered, but that was all she could say about it. A pile of discarded car parts lay close to the house, trees growing through and around them. Beside them sat an old washing machine, red with rust. Beyond that were three car bodies. Empty plastic pails and rags and bottles were heaped beside the rickety step to the house. The roofline sagged, and one window was boarded up. Rebecca suddenly understood Joe's reluctance to take this over. It would take a lot of work just to clean up. She hated to think what the rest of the place looked like.

Rebecca did a quarter turn and caught her breath. The mountains seemed closer than before, imposing and overwhelming. She shook her head, bemused at her reaction. She had seen mountains on four continents, had skied in some of them and just enjoyed the others. But these mountains rising from the plains were special to her.

The land flowed here. Golden prairie, hills edged with deep green, purple mountains sharply outlined against a sky of an impossible blue. It created a sense of rightness, of serenity and harmony.

Whatever the rest of the yard was, the view more than made up for it.

Rebecca turned and carefully made her way up the stairs to the house, testing each step as she went. She knocked on the metal door, the tinny sound echoing. There was no answer. After a decent interval, she con-

cluded that no one was home. Well, she had tried.
She was surprised at her disappointment. She turned
to leave, looking once more at the view.

As she did, she noticed a horse and rider cantering
down the hill, small puffs of dust following each fall
of the horse's hooves.

Rebecca walked toward her vehicle, watching. The
horse's legs moved in an even rhythm, effortlessly
closing the gap between the horse and the yard. It had
to be Joe, she thought with a lift to her heart.

Even from here she could see how one hand rested
on his thigh. The other held the reins loosely. He
looked far more relaxed sitting on the loping horse
than he had in the chair across from her at the bank.

As he came closer, Rebecca realized with a start of
fear that he was coming right up to her.

She took a quick step toward her vehicle, trying to
put it between her and the oncoming horse. Her limp
hampered her. The snorting of the horse, the rhythmic
thump of his hooves came closer. Rebecca stifled her
panic as Joe pulled up on the other side of her truck.
With a grin, he vaulted easily off the horse. Rebecca
forced herself to take a steadying breath and to ignore
the large animal that was only ten feet away from her.

"Hi, there," he said, pulling off his cowboy hat.
He brushed his hand off on his shirt and walked
around the car, leading the horse.

But his easy grin didn't dispel the sudden feeling
of panic that gripped Rebecca at the sight of the
horse's rolling eyes and heaving flanks, the harsh

sound of her labored breath. An image, unbidden, flashed through her mind. Hooves in the air, the squeal of a horse. And then nothing.

Rebecca hoped her hand wasn't trembling as she took Joe's. She hated the lack of control, hated the unwanted memories. She glanced at him, then away. "So you made it," she said. The words sounded inane and limp coming from a chest that was pounding in a mixture of fear and anxiety.

Joe dipped his head forward as if to catch her eye, his mouth lifting in a lazy half-grin. "You picked a good day."

She nodded, not trusting herself to speak, wishing he would take the horse away, angry at her own weakness.

"So, do you want to have a look around?" Joe set his hat on his head.

She steadied her breathing, nodded but didn't move. Couldn't move.

"Is something wrong, Rebecca?" He stood in front of her, his head tilted, his voice wary.

She looked at him and saw the concern in his expression. She knew she didn't have the strength to take even a single step. If she did, she would fall. That would be too humiliating.

"Rebecca, you look pale. What's the matter?"

"It's your horse," she blurted, unable to stop herself. "He makes me nervous." Now that's an understatement, she thought as she swallowed a bubble of fear.

Joe frowned and looked at the huge animal that now stood, her head lowered as she worked at the bit in her mouth. Joe looked carefully at her as understanding dawned. "Does it have anything to do with your injury?"

Rebecca held her hand against her throat, as if to coax extra air into it, as if to draw out the events of that day. "Yes."

Joe nodded, turned and walked the horse to the corrals. As Rebecca watched the animal leave, she felt a wave of trembling flow through her. Reaction, she thought, taking a deep breath. Then another.

Joe tied up the horse and came to stand in front of her.

"Are you okay?" he asked quietly. The air around them was hushed, broken only by the occasional whicker from the horse, the far-off trill of blackbirds. Even the soft wind had stopped, and stillness fell around them. Rebecca felt as if cold fingers were squeezing her temple. She closed her eyes as memories came crashing into her mind. She clenched her fist as if in defense against them, but once again she heard the scream of a horse, saw wide eyes and flaring nostrils. She stood quietly, waiting for the edge to wear off, for the fear to subside.

Then she felt Joe's hand resting lightly on her shoulder, as if ready to catch her.

"You should sit down," he said. "You look as though you're going to faint." Joe held out his other hand to her.

Rebecca let him take her hand, his large one engulfing hers as he slowly led her up the walk. Her legs felt wobbly, and she was thankful for his strong arm supporting her.

For a moment she thought he was going to take her into the dingy home, but he led her around the house to a secluded spot sheltered by trees. An old picnic table sat in the shade, its paint peeling. But it looked solid.

"Here, sit down. I'll see if Lane has anything in the house."

"No." Rebecca caught his arm. "No, please don't. It's okay. I'm fine," she said with a shaky laugh, reaching for control, embarrassed. "I don't know what came over me just then. Silly, really."

Joe sat beside her, his large hands holding hers. "Silly doesn't exactly cover the way you looked," he said wryly.

Rebecca took slow, deep breaths, wishing the trembling would stop. How she hated these moments of weakness. To have one happen in front of Joe was doubly hard.

"Take your time," he said quietly, massaging her ice cold hands with his warm ones.

Rebecca nodded, looking away from a pair of soft brown eyes tinged with concern. She couldn't take that right now. Not from him.

"Can I ask what happened?" Joe asked softly.

Rebecca looked at their hands, unwilling to pull away, her heart's tempo increasing once again. She didn't want to tell him, but it was as if the words were forced out of her. "When I saw you with your horse, it all came back."

"What did?" Joe's voice was quiet, almost soothing.

Rebecca shrugged. "All I remember is a horse rearing, screaming—" Her voice broke as she struggled to reconstruct the events. "I had a fight with my boyfriend, Kyle. He was angry. Yelling. The horse got frightened and reared." She stared past Joe as pictures coalesced, finding substance in her retelling. "I ran away and then Kyle came after me. On the horse." More images, other emotions. Anxiety as the hoofbeats of the horse quickened. Turning slowly to see Kyle coming after her. Then the hooves of the horse off to one side, falling, falling as if in slow motion. "The horse landed on me," she said quietly, amazed at her control as unwanted memories slid back. "Right on me."

Joe squeezed her hands, offering comfort. "How long ago did this happen?" Joe's voice was quiet in the absolute stillness.

Rebecca looked at his large hand covering hers, the blunt fingernails, the faint lines of grease that stained his fingers. She allowed the contact for a few moments more, then with a sigh pulled away, reality bringing with it the knowledge that she was supposed to be here on business. Joe was a customer. She was his loans officer. She didn't even know why she was telling him all this. Telling him things she had only told a few people.

"A year," she replied, carefully.

"And the boyfriend?" Joe's question was quiet, but she could hear an edge of anger in it. She looked at him, puzzled why it should matter to him.

"Right after the accident, Kyle went east to take a job there," she said, drawing in a cleansing breath, willing away the last vestiges of emotion that Kyle's name had created. "I haven't heard from him since."

"What about you," he asked, "were you riding, as well?"

Rebecca shook her head as the memories settled. "No. I was walking."

"How did you get to the hospital?"

"I don't remember." She chanced a look at him. His posture was casual, but his eyes were narrowed. "All I remember is seeing his horse slide then fall, and the next thing I knew I woke up in the hospital."

"Who owned the horse?"

"Kyle. He didn't ride it much. It was more of a pet than a horse. I still don't know why it acted that way."

"A lot of people forget a horse is a pet that can kill you with one well-placed kick." Joe leaned forward, his eyes intent.

Rebecca sat back, surprised at the intensity of his voice. "Kyle used to ride more often. He wasn't a rank amateur, but it was a purebred Arabian and a bit high-strung."

Joe blinked then with a short laugh sat back. "Sorry. I tend to get a little preachy when it comes to how some people treat their horses." He rested one elbow on the table, his hand dangling close to hers. "How long had he had his horse?"

"It was his graduation present."

"Mustn't have been very well-trained."

"It should be. It came from some fancy place in Kentucky. They flew it into Calgary."

Joe ran his finger lightly up and down her hand. His gentle touch relaxed her. "So they didn't pick it up from the local auction market," he said.

Rebecca laughed, surprised she could. Talking about Kyle had always made her bitter and angry, but with Joe it felt different. "It was a pretty expensive horse. Kyle was always going on about its bloodlines, like I cared," Rebecca conceded. "I liked my graduation present better, anyhow."

"And that was?"

Rebecca shrugged, realizing she sounded as if she was bragging. "Doesn't matter."

"Satisfy my curiosity," he said softly, his finger still lightly caressing her hand.

She didn't want to, but his voice was compelling.

"I got a new sports car. Dad traded it in on the truck when I graduated from university."

"That's a hardship," he said with a grin.

"It was his idea, not mine."

"Well your truck is faster than a horse, although maybe not as reliable."

"Hey, it got here." She smiled at him, thankful for the levity his comments had brought to the atmosphere. "And what did you get for graduation?"

Joe lifted his shoulder in a nonchalant shrug, grinning at her. "Honey, I didn't even graduate. As soon as I could I dropped out, got my trucker's license and only looked back to see if I could switch lanes."

Rebecca was taken aback at his admission. And his smile, as if he didn't seem to mind, as if he was almost proud of it. "Do you regret it?"

Joe pursed his lips and shook his head. "Nah. I probably got more education working out in the real world than a lot of kids get in university. I saved money and I got a start. And now, if things go the way you and Dale have planned, I'll be taking over this." Joe waved his hand toward the yard and all its junk. "Quite the estate, isn't it?"

Rebecca said nothing, hearing beneath his light-hearted comment a hint of embarrassment.

"Did you still want the grand tour?" He lifted his eyebrows.

Rebecca looked at her steady hands, taking in a breath to calm a suddenly trembling heart.

"We can avoid the horse," he added. "And I'll be right beside you."

Why that final assurance made all the difference to Rebecca, she didn't stop to ponder. "Okay," she said, slowly getting to her feet. "Let's go, then."

The tour of the yard didn't take long. Rebecca

wasn't a farm girl, but she knew how to assess buildings. They all needed work, as did the corrals.

Joe pointed out things he had done while he was living on the ranch and what he thought needed to be done yet. In spite of his jovial manner, Rebecca could tell that the condition of the yard bothered him.

They had come to her vehicle, a good distance from the quiet horse.

"Do you have a bit of time yet?" Joe asked as Rebecca pulled her keys from the pocket of her pants. "I'd like to show you my place."

Rebecca felt a curious lift of her heart at the words. His place. It created a gentle intimacy.

"It's not far," he added quickly. "You go back to the road then over about three-quarters of a mile. Mine is the first place south. It will take you almost as long to drive there as it will take me to ride."

"Okay," she replied, reasoning that it would be helpful to have an idea of what his yard looked like. "I'll meet you there, then."

Joe grinned. "We'll see who gets there first."

Rebecca laughed. "You're on."

Chapter Eight

Rebecca had beat him, but not by much, thought Joe as he came over the hill. She had parked by his truck and was just getting out when he rode onto the yard.

She stayed back while he unsaddled Mack and put him in the pen. Then he walked to Rebecca.

Joe slowed his steps to keep pace with her, making sure he took an easy path to the corrals, proud of how neat and orderly they were. As they passed the vehicles, he couldn't help but glance sidelong at hers. It was probably worth more than his mobile home and truck combined, he thought. With possibly one or two of the horses thrown in.

Graduation present, he thought, incredulous, unable to imagine anyone with enough money to simply saunter down to the local car dealership and trade up to one of the newest vehicles on the market just because a daughter graduated from university.

He pushed the sleeves of his worn cotton shirt to his elbows, glancing at her as he did so. He guessed from the way her sleeveless tunic draped and moved with the slightest breeze that it was high quality. Probably pure silk.

She was new vehicles and first-class trips abroad, he was thrift stores and the occasional drive to Calgary in his dented pickup. She was silk and he was worn cotton.

She was rich and he was poor.

He wondered once again at the wisdom of letting her see for herself just how little he really had. Back there, on what he still thought of as his father's place, he had an urge to show her what he had accomplished on his own. Compared to his father's ranch, his was organized, neat and clean. But now, seeing it through her eyes, it suddenly looked poor and shabby.

So why was he looking at her, noticing her, hoping she would smile at him again? Why was he wishing she would tilt her head and turn those exotic blue eyes towards him, let that mouth lift in a smile that transformed her face from beautiful to breathtaking?

Joe shook his head at his fancy. She had shown him an intimate part of herself, but what did that mean? He just happened to catch her in an unguarded moment.

"How much land did you say your brother leased?" Rebecca was breathless, and Joe turned his attention to her. Her limp was more noticeable, and it seemed to cause her some difficulty.

Joe told her, then slowed. "We don't have to do this," he said, hoping she wouldn't agree. His misplaced pride had brought her here. He wondered again why she had agreed to come.

"I'm fine." Her voice was tight, and Joe sensed embarrassment. He began praying for her, praying her fear would subside, praying he could help her.

They were nearing the horse paddocks when Rebecca slowed. Then, without saying a word, she reached out to Joe.

Silently he took her outstretched hand, tucked it in the crook of his arm and pulled her close, a sudden urge to protect her coming over him, a feeling of rightness in the way she leaned on him and the way he supported her.

Together they walked toward the horses.

Talia was in the first paddock.

"This is my stake horse, or was." Joe laughed shortly as he brought Rebecca closer. "She got injured when my renter was looking after her."

"What happened?" Rebecca sounded breathless, and her hand clutched his arm.

"She got scared and jumped a barbed wire fence."

"Scared?" Rebecca glanced sidelong at Joe, then at Talia.

"Yeah." Joe smiled as he looked from Rebecca to Talia, who stood watching them warily, her head down, expressing her submission. "Another horse was after her, showing her who was boss, and Talia tried to run away. You always have to be careful when you bring a new horse into an established bunch. They have a definite pecking order, and Talia was a threat to the order.''

''Because she's so big?''

''No. Because she was new.'' Joe clucked to Talia, who raised her head and took a few halting steps forward. ''You can see the stitches on the side of her leg now.''

Talia turned her head sideways, as if studying them, but didn't come any closer. Her wound was healing nicely, but it was still a raw slash on her sleek hide, a disfigurement on a once beautiful and proud animal.

''Why is she doing that?'' asked Rebecca, still holding tightly to Joe's arm. ''Turning her head like that?''

''Horses don't have the same kind of vision we have,'' Joe explained, one hand covering Rebecca's, pulling her closer. He didn't think about it—it was an automatic response to an unspoken request on her part. ''Because our eyes are side by side, we have good depth perception and can focus instantly. A horse has what's called monocular vision. They can see far away but not so well up close.'' While he was talking he took a step closer to the pen, and Rebecca followed. ''They flee from a threat and then analyze from a distance. As well, horses were created to live in wide-open spaces. I usually give my horses a run outside, but I'm still keeping an eye on her. I don't want her to injure herself any more. So she's a little more wary because her key survival mechanism, flight, is taken away from her.''

As he spoke, he felt Rebecca's hand clutch his arm less tightly. She seemed to relax. ''Horses and people have been created quite different, and in order to work with a horse you have to understand her. When we're not communicating, then I run into problems. It's not always the horse's fault.'' Joe moved Rebecca closer to the fence and, still holding her arm, laid one hand along the top rail. ''My horses usually want to please me. They're not out to hurt me, and if they do it's because I was unfortunately in the way.''

''Isn't there such a thing as a mean horse?'' Rebecca's voice was quiet, almost strained, but Joe took her question as a positive response.

He glanced at Rebecca, pleased to see the tightness gone from around her mouth. He wanted her to see the horses through his eyes. It bothered him that she was afraid of an animal he cared so much for. ''If horses are mean,'' he replied, ''it's because something happened somewhere along the way that broke a trust, or someone let the horse have its way too often.''

Rebecca took a hesitant step closer, eyeing Talia, who wove back and forth at the end of the pen. Joe clucked to her, and her head came up. Another cluck brought her hesitantly closer to the fence.

''Can I get her to come closer?'' Joe asked, turning to Rebecca.

Rebecca nodded once, taking a deep breath.

Joe squeezed her hand in encouragement, another cluck brought Talia's head over the fence. "Good girl," Joe said, praising her, petting her neck. "You are such a sweetheart, aren't you?" he said, stroking her head, rubbing her under her chin. Talia stood quietly, turning her head to Rebecca.

"You can touch her if you want," Joe encouraged.

Rebecca reached out hesitantly, touching Talia's nose. Talia immediately nudged her.

"Next time she does that, smack the side of her neck," instructed Joe.

"Why?" Rebecca drew back, puzzled.

"At first encounter, horses try to establish pecking order—to find out who's boss. No offence, but she sees you as another horse, or at least someone to try out."

"But all she did was nudge me. Maybe she wants something?"

Joe shrugged. "Probably does. But the deal with horses is they're always trying to figure out who's in charge. You didn't ask her to nuzzle you like that, did you?"

"No."

"So, then don't let her do that. Even something as simple as a nuzzle is a space invasion on the part of the horse, a very insignificant challenge. With horses, you're the boss."

Rebecca had let go of Joe and had both her hands on the top of the fence, watching Talia as if seeing her through different eyes. "So what do I do?"

"Next time she comes close to you and tries to nudge you like that, you have three seconds to let her know that it isn't welcome."

"Why three seconds?" Rebecca turned to Joe, a light smile teasing her mouth. "Is that a rule?"

Joe smiled and winked. "Horses have a short attention span. If you do anything after that she won't know what you were doing it for."

Rebecca nodded and turned her attention to Talia, who stood back, her head turned toward them, her ears perked forward.

Joe laid his arms on the fence, his chin resting on his stacked hands, his head tilted so he could watch Rebecca. A soft spring breeze riffled through the yard, teasing Rebecca's hair, lifting it from her face. She looked more relaxed than she had before, and Joe sent up a prayer of thanks.

"How many horses do you have?" Rebecca asked.

"Four of my own and two that I'm working with for some other clients."

"How did you start with this?" Rebecca looked around then at Joe.

"I was always fooling with horses. Just had a natural aptitude for it. I got a lot of help from a good friend, Allister McLure. He's the local vet. He's also the one who started me going to church. I had two horses when I was in high school. I entered some cutting horse competitions with a couple of them. Won a few prizes."

"And what happened to them?"

Joe's lips tightened as he remembered far too well the farm auction, the ignominy of having classmates' parents purchasing his trained animals for less than they were worth just so his father could cover his mistakes. "They're gone now," he said shortly. He looked at Rebecca, wondering what she would say if he told her the details of his past, wondered if she would be able to understand what he had lived with.

"That must have been hard," she said quietly. "Where is your father now?"

Joe looked beyond the corrals, not seeing them. Remembering a funeral, remembering his feelings of guilt. "He died four years ago."

Rebecca looked away. "I'm sorry," she said quietly.

"It took me awhile before I was truly sorry. I didn't get along with him very well. He got in an accident down in Mexico, and I went down with Lane to see him. But I barely got to speak with him before he died."

"That's hard," she said, turning to walk away.

Joe didn't want her to go. He wanted her to stay, to talk to him. He wanted to find out more about her. "Do you have any other brothers or sisters besides Jenna?"

Rebecca shook her head. "No. Just Jenna. She's enough sister for me."

"What do you mean?"

"I love Jenna a lot, but she tends to be overprotective." Rebecca smiled at Joe as if to apologize for what she said. "She has definite ideas of what I should and shouldn't be doing. She hovers and fusses and tries to make sure I don't overexert myself. My mother and Jenna would like nothing better than if I would quit my job and stay at home."

"I can't see you doing that."

Rebecca's gaze shot to his, her head tilted as if she was studying him. "You can't?"

"No. You seem to be a very determined person."

She smiled. "Thanks, Joe. I take that as a compliment." She looked away again. "My mother always said that, too, but somehow coming from her it was a reprimand. My dear mother is of the firm belief that my limp would be greatly reduced if I pray more."

"Do you?"

Rebecca was quiet, and Joe regretted the question. But somehow he wanted to know, needed to find out what and how she believed.

"I used to pray more. I used to think that if I just say the words enough times God will heal me. I used all the right praying formulas and quoted all the Bible passages. My parents prayed, my sister prayed, my grandparents prayed. The church I belonged to prayed." She clutched her hands together. "After a while I realized that I was wasting my time. God knew everything I was telling Him. He knew what my heart's desire was. But nothing has changed."

Silence drifted between them as Joe wondered what he could tell her that she hadn't heard before. He hadn't been a Christian long enough that he felt he could give her any kind of spiritual advice. Especially not when she spoke so easily of her family, her parents and grandparents and their prayers. But he heard a bitter note in her voice that jarred when she spoke of God. "You talk about God like He doesn't matter to you."

"I still believe in God, Joe Brewer," Rebecca said quietly, easing some of his disquiet. "Just in case you think that I've turned my back on Him because of some minor disability." She looked at him, her mouth curved in a wry smile. "I just know that some things aren't as important to Him as they are to me."

Joe nodded, aware of a vague discomfort he couldn't quite put his finger on. "Shouldn't your prayer be more than asking?" he pressed on.

Rebecca blinked, hesitating. "I've spent an entire life praying to God, being obedient and doing what I was supposed to. And I know that my prayers should be more than just a listing of please and thank-you, but I also know that lately it's getting harder and harder for me."

"To ask for anything?"

Rebecca rubbed one hand over the other. "To pray, period."

"What about just conversation?"

Rebecca looked at him and frowned. "Excuse me?"

"What about just talking to God. A conversation."

Rebecca straightened. "A conversation requires response. That's where things fall apart for me, Joe. I know that I'm slowly praying less and caring less. It scares me, but it seems I can't do much about it."

Joe was silent. He didn't know what to say to her, what words he could pull out that would restore her faith.

Rebecca looked at her wristwatch. "Oh, my." She glanced at Joe. "I'm sorry. I've taken up most of your time going on about my own personal problems, and I'm sure you have more important things to do."

Joe tilted his head, looking at her, suddenly seeing a measure of vulnerability that her expensive clothes and composed manner couldn't hide. And he realized that in spite of her words, her faith was stronger than she let on. He wanted her to stay. He wanted to talk more about her faith, about his faith. He wanted to give her what little he could. That she had opened up to him, that she had shared her doubts with him had created a bond he wanted to strengthen.

"I'm glad you came," he said quietly.

Rebecca looked at him, smiling. "I'm glad I came, too." She tilted her head, studying him. "I've been taught from the Bible since I was a young child. I've studied and been taught in school. But when I hear you talk, I hear a sincerity and peace that I know I've been missing. I envy you that."

"And I envy you your praying parents and grand-parents. You have a heritage that I've never had. My parents never went to church, and I became a Christian because of a vet named Allister who loved horses, too. Your faith in God is rooted in you. I don't think you can walk away from that so easily.''

Rebecca pressed her lips together and looked away. Surreptitiously she reached up and swiped at her cheek.

He wanted to take her in his arms and reassure her. He wanted to pray with her, to show her that everything she had ever had was still there. But he didn't have the right.

A light breeze had rearranged her hair, dropping strands of it over her face. Without stopping to think, he reached over and carefully brushed them away, just as her own hand came up. Their fingers met, then his hand twined around hers, holding it gently, carefully, as if afraid that she would pull back.

But she didn't. Instead she smiled shakily, and his heart skipped as she slowly turned her head toward his hand, her eyes drifting shut.

Joe swallowed, his hand curving around the silky softness of her cheek. ''I want to see you again, Rebecca.'' He waited to see what she would say, but she was silent. She hadn't laughed and she hadn't said no, so he pressed on. ''Are you busy Friday night?''

She slowly dropped his hand and looked away. ''I'm sorry,'' she said, ''I have a date.'' Her words pushed him ever so gently into his place. He shouldn't have been surprised.

''Dale,'' he said with a short laugh at his presumptions.

She nodded, her eyes unable to meet his. "But I'd like to see you. Some other time, maybe?"

"Sure," he said. She would say that, he figured. Best way to let a guy down easy was to make some nebulous plans for "some other time." He had done it enough. He recognized the method. Besides, he knew he didn't stand a chance against a guy who worked in a bank and whose parents owned three hardware stores.

"I'd better go." Rebecca paused, as if she was going to say something else, then, with a shake of her head, turned and slowly walked toward her vehicle.

Joe stayed behind, watching her progress, ready to come running if she stumbled. But she didn't. She got into the truck, tossed him a wave, then turned and left him in a cloud of dust.

Well, Lord, he prayed, I guess that was a message loud and clear. He sighed as he watched her leave. Then he turned and went to his horses.

Chapter Nine

Rebecca smiled politely at Dale and looked around the restaurant. Soft music played in the background— a string quartet, for goodness sakes. They had finished their meal awhile ago, but Dale wanted to linger.

Rebecca toyed with the heavy silver fork she had used to eat her cheesecake. It hardly made a sound on the thick damask tablecloth. Centered on the ivory cloth were a crystal bowl, cut flowers and a candle floating in an amber liquid.

"I think I like the ambience here much better than the restaurant we went to last week," Dale said, looking around, satisfied with himself.

"It is a very nice place," Rebecca agreed. It would be petty to say otherwise. From the carved frame-and-panel oak walls to the curved ceiling with its ornate plasterwork and chandelier dripping with crystal, it bespoke subdued wealth and affluence.

But to Rebecca, it didn't seem to matter where they went. All Dale's choices had the same feeling of stiltedness, the same smothering decor, the same disciplined politeness on the parts of the waiters or waitresses.

And tonight, after an emotionally draining day, all Rebecca wanted to do was stay home and sleep, but Jenna wouldn't hear of it.

"I was hoping we could come here again next Friday." Dale leaned forward, smiling. "I have tickets for the symphony afterward."

Dinner and the symphony? Rebecca almost groaned. The evening sounded like most evenings she and her parents spent when she was younger. At first they had been fun, but after she had sat through seventeen different renditions of Rachmaninoff and the incomprehensible music of countless modern composers, the events became a chore.

Rebecca smiled politely while her brain scrambled for an excuse. The idea of such an evening was enough to make her want to scream.

Except well-bred young ladies don't scream. The only option available to them was evasiveness or outright lies. "I think I'm busy that evening," she said quietly.

She could quick enough make the fib a truth, thought Rebecca, thinking about the work she had to do at the bank.

"I'll have to double-check," she continued, still

uncomfortable with her fabrication, "but I'm pretty sure I already have plans."

Dale looked disappointed, and Rebecca felt a flash of guilt. Dale was kind and considerate, and certainly good-looking. But his company just didn't inspire the spark that Rebecca's romantic heart longed for.

An image of intense brown eyes danced in her mind, but Rebecca pushed that picture aside, as well. What was wrong with her? To even entertain the thought of Joe Brewer. She had seen him with so many women. He could never be seriously interested in her. Not the way she was now.

"I guess we'll have to try again sometime," Dale said hopefully. "Will you be in church on Sunday?"

Rebecca nodded, feeling cornered. Jenna would jump at a chance to have Dale over after the service, especially if she found out her sister had turned down a date with him.

Dale smiled and signaled to the waiter that they were ready to leave.

On the drive home, Rebecca laid her head back, pretending to sleep. She didn't want to make small talk. If things had gone the way she planned, she would have canceled the date.

Rebecca had seen the physiotherapist that morning. Heather had frowned and stretched and assessed, and the outcome of the appointment was that things weren't progressing as quickly as Rebecca had hoped.

Rebecca came home to a letter from the last school she had applied to. Its message was terse. "Thanks, but no thanks. Position filled." It wasn't a huge surprise, but oh, how it hurt.

However, she was unable to follow that train of thought. Dale was feeling chatty, asking about her work, her parents, her interests. Rebecca dutifully answered, making sure she asked him questions, as well. The conversation stayed on the surface, a careful discovering of each other. The first time they had gone out they had begun the process. Now she sensed he wanted to get to know her better, but she saw no real future to this relationship, and she didn't feel like going through the motions.

"So how long do you figure on staying in Wakely?" he asked her after another silent interval.

"I'm not sure." Rebecca folded her hands in her lap, pressing her thumbs against each other. "The job is temporary. I imagine I'll leave once the regular loans officer comes back from maternity leave."

Dale nodded. "Do you think you'll ever do anything with your degree?"

Rebecca stifled the pain his question brought up. Not now, she thought. Don't go there now. Not after today. "I don't know." That was all she said, her hands squeezing each other as she tried to maintain some semblance of control.

"I imagine your disability would be a hindrance."

Disability. Hindrance. Such nice, comfortable words that skated over the surface without really saying anything.

"May I ask how it happened?" he continued.

Rebecca pressed her lips together, taking slow, shallow breaths. "I'm sorry," she said finally. "I can't talk about it right now."

"No, don't apologize," he said turning to her. "I'm sorry. I shouldn't have pried. It isn't really my business." Rebecca granted her forgiveness with a wan smile, then turned her head and laid it against the seat. She stared out the window, seeing only a muted reflection of her face as she wondered why she couldn't tell Dale what she had so easily confided to Joe.

"Let us bow our heads in a moment of silent prayer, a time for each of us to send out individual petitions to the Lord." The minister directed his friendly smile around the congregation and then lowered his head.

Individual petitions, the minister had said. Rebecca twisted her fingers around each other as she drew in a deep breath. She was tired of praying over a leg that consistently disappointed her.

Instead, she looked surreptitiously over the congregation, trying to find Joe. She had spotted him when she sat down, and if she shifted herself just so, she could catch a glimpse of him across the aisle, one pew ahead of where she sat.

He was leaning forward, his elbows on his knees, his hands folded with his thumbs resting against his forehead. His eyes were shut tight, and as Rebecca watched, she wondered what he was praying for, wondering if Joe Brewer was doing what he suggested she do. Simply talking to God. As she watched, she saw a soft smile tease the corner of his mouth, deepening a dimple in his cheek.

She wondered what he was smiling about. What about his prayer could have created the sense of peace that surrounded him? She remembered last Sunday and the unmistakable devotion he had shown then. His faith seemed to be an integral part of him, yet as she thought of how women were so obviously attracted to him, it didn't fit.

The organist played a soft doxology, signaling an end to the prayer. Rebecca quickly glanced down, hoping no one noticed her lapse. Staring at handsome men when she should be praying. Thinking about Joe when there were myriad requests she could have made on other people's behalf.

God knew, she reasoned, justifying her lack. Nothing she could tell Him was new. He saw and heard everything, including her struggles with physio.

Rebecca slowly stood for the last song, making sure she didn't put any weight on her bad leg until she was sure it would hold, not collapse. Sighing, she opened the hymnal. As the organist started, she looked sideways once more, only to catch Joe looking directly at her. He sent her a hesitant smile that made her breath catch. She couldn't stop her answering smile, couldn't stop the increasing tempo of her heart.

Jenna nudged her, Joe turned and Rebecca glanced at the hymnal, ignoring her sister, who would be frowning her disapproval. Rebecca knew exactly what Jenna thought of Joe. What Rebecca wasn't so sure of were her own thoughts of the man. She found the verse they were singing.

"Shun not suffering pain or loss, help us Lord to bear our cross." Rebecca came to the end of the verse and couldn't stop the closing of her throat. She shut her eyes, fighting for control. She didn't want to cry, but as she thought about the increase in her exercises, the constant hard work, the wondering if it would help, she was scared.

What if her leg was getting worse? What if she lost all her mobility? Wasn't it bad enough that she could barely cross a room without drawing so many curious glances? Or could no longer play the sports she used to enjoy?

She bit her lip, drawing on years of training by her mother, years of maintaining an appearance of composure. It was getting harder.

Rebecca sighed, putting down her spiritual malaise to a general dissatisfaction with her life. Much as she liked being with Jenna and Troy, she found it difficult to work up enthusiasm for her job.

Jenna was nudging her again, and Rebecca realized that the service was over and that people were getting ready to file out.

She dropped her hymnal into the slot, letting her worries go with it. She looked up and saw Joe. He faced forward, holding onto the pew in front of him, his head bent. Rebecca watched as he lifted his head with a smile then turned to her. She couldn't look away.

"We're waiting for you, Rebecca," Jenna said from behind.

"Sorry." Rebecca stepped into the aisle to allow Jenna to go past.

"Go ahead, Becks," Jenna said, urging her forward.

"No. I'll just hold you up," she said.

Jenna frowned, but Shannon was dragging on her arm. She had no choice but to walk past her sister.

"Hello, Rebecca." The deep voice speaking her name from behind her made Rebecca's heart skip a beat. She half turned to Joe, unable to stop her smile of greeting. "How are you doing?" he asked, returning her smile.

"I'm fine, thanks," she said, hoping she didn't sound as breathless as she felt, suddenly tongue-tied around him. She caught the first thought that entered her mind. "How's your horse? The one that was hurt."

"She's doing good." Joe grinned as he sidestepped a little girl who insisted on going past them. "I had her out yesterday for awhile."

Rebecca nodded, aware of how self-conscious she felt around him and wondering what had happened to her usual composure.

They walked on in silence, Rebecca aware that her slow steps were holding up the people behind them. But Joe continued looking casual and relaxed.

"And how was your date on Friday?" he asked as they finally reached the double doors leading outside.

Rebecca felt her neck go warm and glanced at him as if to see if he was mocking her, but his expression was serious. As she looked at him, the hint of a dimple in his cheek, the softness of his eyes, she wondered what a date with him would entail. Most certainly not a fancy dinner and the symphony. "It was okay," was all she said, unwilling to be unfair to Dale, yet also unwilling to let Joe think she had the time of her life.

"I imagine Dale's going to be taking up your weekends more often," he suggested, glancing at her.

"I don't think so." The words came out quickly, as if of their own will. Rebecca bit her lip, wondering what had come over her, wondering what he would think. "Last night was probably our last date."

"What do you mean by that?" Joe's voice was quiet. Had she imagined the hopeful note in it? She tried to find the right answer as they paused at the top of the stairs.

"Oh, Joe, there you are." A young woman with short blond hair waved to Joe. Rebecca recognized Stephanie from last week.

Rebecca clung to the banister as she watched the woman come toward them. Stephanie easily ran up the stairs to Joe. She threaded her arm through his, and Rebecca felt a shaft of envy pierce her hard and deep.

"I was looking for you, Joe," Stephanie said

breathlessly. "Some of the youth group want to go horseback riding, and we need a couple of extra horses. I thought maybe you had some you could spare."

"I think I could, Stephanie." Joe glanced at Rebecca as if to say something to her.

"We're talking about leaving on Friday and coming back Saturday." Stephanie continued chatting, easily drawing Joe from Rebecca.

Rebecca was left standing at the top of the stairs. Her heart began a slow thudding. She couldn't keep her eyes off the young woman, her short skirt, her perfect long legs, her ease with Joe.

Why should that matter? she asked herself. Joe Brewer is the last person you should be daydreaming about. He's popular with a dozen women, but his prospects aren't great.

The reasons were valid, but as she listed them, another part of her preferred to remember his attentiveness, the gentle touch of his hand, his deep and quiet voice as he talked about his horses, his plans, his faith.

But reality made short work of her daydreams as she clenched her teeth and forced herself to concentrate on getting down the stairs without mishap. The church had a ramp for handicapped people, but she absolutely refused to use it, preferring to take her chances with the stairs. Just as she moved her leg the next step, she felt it. Just a light twinge in her thigh, but it sent a wave of dread through her body. That's how the muscle spasms started. With an innocent squeeze, a light reminder before the cramping knots seized her leg in their painful, paralyzing grip. Not now, not again, she thought, closing her eyes in desperation. Please, Lord, not again, not after all the hard work. She opened her eyes and took a steadying breath. She didn't know why she had prayed. Instinct, she figured.

Jenna caught up with her. "Are you okay? You look a little pale."

"I'm fine, Jenna." Rebecca struggled to keep her voice even, to keep emotion out of it. She forced herself to concentrate on external things. How the sun shone in the sky. How she had just come out of church. How Easter was coming, when all things would be made new.

"I saw you talking to Joe...." Jenna let the sentence hang, waiting for Rebecca to fill in the rest.

But Rebecca didn't feel like playing Jenna's little game. Instead she glanced once over her shoulder, looking for him, but he was gone.

"Let's go, Becks. Dinner's waiting," Jenna reminded her sister.

Rebecca nodded and followed without another backward glance.

At home, Rebecca helped Jenna in the kitchen. Jenna had done much of the preparation that morning, and quickly they had everything on the table in the dining nook off the kitchen.

Jenna called the children and her husband. As they all settled around the table, she smiled around the group, a contented mother hen with all her chicks around her.

Including me, thought Rebecca with a wry smile as she took Shannon's hand for prayer. They bent their heads, and Troy asked for a blessing on the food, thanking the Lord for the blessings of the day, for church and home and family. He paused at the end of the prayer, allowing each of them a chance to pray her own prayer. Rebecca felt herself go still, felt as if words in her were waiting to be voiced, as if God was waiting for her.

But she didn't know what to say, so she kept her mind blank.

The prayer was over, and lunch began.

"I noticed you were talking to Joe Brewer after church today," Jenna said again as she spooned soup for her family.

Rebecca nodded, handing a bowl to her niece. She knew her question at church had not been forgotten, only forestalled.

"I was checking out his place the other day. He's applied for a loan." Rebecca gave her sister full marks for persistence and wondered what she really wanted.

"I heard he has plans of buying his brother's ranch."

"Joe's a good, solid young man with a good head

on his shoulders. I don't doubt he'll make a go of the place," Troy said.

Rebecca shot him a look. She was surprised at Troy's unexpected support. In the office, he never said much about the people he had known since his youth, and what he said about Joe gave her an unexpected thrill.

"He doesn't even have a high school diploma. How can he have a good head on his shoulders?" Jenna snorted. She took a cookie out of her daughter's hands. "No, have a few carrots and some soup first," she admonished.

"There's lot of successful businesspeople who never finished school," said Rebecca, encouraged by Troy's remarks. "Dale's father only had a grade six education. He did quite well." She avoided Jenna's angry look, crumbling some crackers in her niece's soup. "I don't know if that's always an indication of anyone's worth."

"Joe's worth is quite low, I might add." Jenna took a spoonful of soup and looked from Rebecca to her husband. "The boy doesn't have two pennies to rub together. I mean, look at that wreck of a trailer he lives in. I'm sure it's falling apart around his ears."

"It's actually quite neat and clean and in pretty decent shape," Rebecca said, her tone more sharp than she intended. She reached across the table for a bun and broke it open, ignoring Jenna's shocked look. "His whole place is well tended. It's obvious he takes good care of what he has." She felt her neck go warm at her defense of Joe, but Jenna's remarks bothered her in many ways.

"And how would you know?" Jenna spoke quietly, but Rebecca could sense the anger in her words.

Rebecca shrugged, trying to look nonchalant. "I told you I had to go there and go over a few things for his loan." She held Jenna's piercing gaze. "I think Troy's right. I think Joe will make a go of whatever he starts."

"Don't tell me," Jenna said, laying down her spoon and leaning forward. "Don't tell me you've become like every other besotted woman in this county. You're falling for Joe Brewer." She turned to Troy. "Can't you assign him another loans officer? She doesn't have to deal with him."

"Jenna, stop it." Against her will, Rebecca felt her neck go warm at Jenna's words. "I'm a trained professional who is doing her job. Visiting clients at their home is part of it."

"And talking to them after church and smiling at them like they're the greatest thing since panty hose is also part of your job?"

Rebecca was taken aback at the anger Jenna showed.

"Jenna, you're getting a little carried away," Troy warned, reaching to lay a gentling hand on his wife's arm.

"No, I'm not." Jenna pulled her arm away, turning to Rebecca. "I've seen how that guy operates. He can't walk down the street but he's flirting with some girl. Walks into church and Stephanie and Rachel are all over him. The shy ones just stare. You watch him, Becks. He's not our kind of people.''

"Jenna, be careful," Troy reprimanded.

In spite of Troy's support, Rebecca felt her back stiffen at what Jenna said. "I thought as Christians, we didn't have a 'kind' of people," she replied, struggling to keep her voice even. She wished she could get up, wished she could escape the resentment she heard in Jenna's voice. The fear.

But it wasn't fair to the girls to make a scene. So she turned away from Jenna. "And what should we do after lunch, Amanda? Do you have a game we can play?"

Amanda nodded, smiling at her aunt. "I like stick-up picks," she replied.

"That's a great game," Rebecca said with a smile.

When lunch was over and Troy read the devotional, Rebecca left with her nieces, leaving Jenna to stew on her own.

Rebecca knew Jenna. She was persistent and tenacious. Rebecca knew she hadn't heard the end of this.

Chapter Ten

⟡

Joe scratched his chin with his index finger as he paused at the doorway to the bank. He shoved his hands in his pockets and glanced over his shoulder as if looking for an escape route.

He turned to the door, remembering that it was Rebecca's oblique comment yesterday about ending her relationship with Dale that brought him to town today. Checking out a secondhand tractor parked at Wilson's Farm Equipment was just an excuse. But as he stood on the sidewalk with the warm spring sun pouring out of the sky, self-doubt beat him on the head. He wondered if he had read more into the situation than he should have.

He turned, leaning against the stucco wall, chewing his lip. Was he crazy? He was a dirt-poor rancher, and she was a spoiled rich girl.

His thoughts went back and forth as he struggled

with what he knew and what he felt. Somehow Rebecca Stevenson had him in her grip, and the best way he knew to handle it was to ask her out, spend time with her, see where it would go.

What do I do, Lord? Do I wait? Do I act? Do I want to set myself up like this?

He shoved his hands in his pockets and pushed away from the building, stopped and turned, almost bumping into Lorna McLure.

"Sorry, Lorna," he said, taking a step back. "I wasn't looking."

"That's okay," she replied, swinging a shopping bag. "I don't often get to bump into handsome young men. I don't mind."

"Give me a break, Lorna," Joe said, unconsciously tilting his head toward her.

She grinned at him. "So what brings you to town on this glorious spring day?"

Joe shrugged and scratched his head. "I had to go to the bank for some business."

"Must be hard business." Lorna gave him a knowing look. "You've been hovering around here for the past few minutes. Are you thinking of asking Rebecca out?"

Joe stifled a groan at her directness. "Was it that obvious?"

Lorna smiled. "You two looked pretty cozy on Sunday."

"All we talked about was my horses and her date with Dale Aiken."

"I don't think you have to worry about Dale and Rebecca. The way she was looking at you, I'm pretty sure he's not that important to her."

Joe hung onto her words, wondering why he needed affirmation of how Rebecca felt about him, but he did. Rebecca Stevenson was slowly turning him inside out, and he didn't know what to do about it.

"So, are you going to go in there and ask her out?" she continued.

Joe ran a hand through his hair and grinned at Lorna, an unusual answer to his prayer of just a few moments ago. "You know, I think I will." He leaned down to give her a quick hug. "I think I just will. Thanks, Lorna."

"I'm pretty sure she'll say yes," she called after him as he pushed open the door and tossed her a parting grin over his shoulder.

But once the door fell shut behind him the aura of the bank surrounded him. The logo on the wall ahead of him had been emblazoned on letters and documents sent to his father, reminding him of outstanding loans. It brought back the choking feeling of debt and squeaking by.

Who did he think he was, asking out a woman who had had more money spent on her in her youth than he had ever seen in his entire life?

You're a child of God, as she is. You share a basic faith in the Lord. That's a better start than any bank account, and you know it. Joe took a deep breath and, trying to disguise his apprehension, sauntered to the reception desk.

Sharla's welcoming grin partly restored his confidence. "Hi, Joe. Dale Aiken is busy. Did you want to wait?"

"No, actually, I want to see Miss Stevenson."

Sharla frowned and looked at a schedule in front of her. "I think she's with another client right now. She should be done any minute."

As Joe hesitated, Troy walked to the desk. "Take any calls for me, Sharla," he said, checking through his messages. "I'm gone for the rest of the day."

"Okay, Mr. Burke."

Troy turned to Joe and held out his hand. "Joe Brewer, how are you doing?"

Joe shook it firmly. "Just fine, thanks."

"Did you want to see me?" Troy glanced at Sharla in confirmation, then at Joe.

"No, he's come to see Miss Stevenson."

Troy nodded, crossing his arms as if taking Joe's measure.

Joe forced himself to look back, reminding himself that not only was this the bank manager who could conceivably hold his fate in his hand, this was also Rebecca's brother-in-law.

"I understand you have quite a bit to discuss with her."

Joe held Troy's steady gaze, wondering what he alluded to, and guessed it was the loan. But he also knew enough about Troy to know that the direct approach was usually the best. "Actually, what I have to discuss with her is of a more personal nature."

"I understand." Troy grinned, and Joe relaxed. "She should be a few minutes." He held Joe's gaze, his own earnest. "Be careful with her."

Joe nodded, a feeling of well-being springing up in him. "I will. Thanks."

The day was looking up, thought Joe. Thank you, Lord, for that confirmation, he prayed as he walked to the reception area.

He wondered about his loan, but pushed the thought aside. The time would come soon enough when he would find out in which direction his business interests were going to move. And he would be given strength to accept that direction.

Joe shoved his hands in his pockets, pacing the carpeted floor. The phone rang in the reception area, and Sharla answered it. "Yes, Miss Stevenson," she said. "I've also got Mr. Brewer here to see you."

Joe's heart skipped at the sound of her name. You've got it bad, Brewer, he thought with a rueful shake of his head.

Sharla looked at him as she hung up the phone. "Miss Stevenson will be right out."

"Thanks." Joe tossed her a disposable smile and continued pacing. What was he going to say to her, he thought, shoving his fingers through his hair. Hi, I was wondering if you'd like to go out with me?

Predictable and boring, made it sound as if he was a high school kid asking her if she wanted to go steady. How about, Are you busy this weekend? Joe groaned. A pickup line if ever there was one.

"Joe? You wanted to see me?"

Rebecca's quiet voice behind him made him whirl. She stood, her delicate hands clasped in front of her, a flowing dove gray dress setting off the blond of her hair, her blue eyes. Her smile was hesitant, as if she wasn't sure why he was here.

Neither am I, thought Joe, swallowing.

"Yeah," he said, then cleared his throat, aware of Sharla, who was watching the proceedings with an open mouth. "I was in town and I, uh, thought maybe we could go out for lunch." Okay, Joe, that was original, he thought, berating himself. She'll fall all over you now.

Rebecca smiled at him. "I'd like that," she said quietly.

Joe frowned, not sure if he heard right. "You would?"

"Yes, I would." Rebecca nodded, and Joe couldn't help his answering smile. "Tell me where you'd like to go, and I'll meet you there," she continued.

"I can wait."

"No. Please. Just tell me where. I don't know exactly how long I'll be."

Joe didn't like the idea but gave in at the concerned look on her face. "I thought we could just go around the corner to Rosie's?"

"Okay. I'll be there in a few minutes."

"Good."

"I have a few things to finish up and then I'll be ready."

"Sure."

She hesitated, then with a puzzled smile, turned and left.

Joe blew out his breath, caught Sharla's surprised gaze and almost blushed. He sounded like some love-struck kid. Well, he thought, maybe I am.

He hadn't been able to put Rebecca Stevenson out of his mind the past few days. He thought about it as he walked out of the bank. He figured he might as well act on it. If he ended up looking slightly foolish in the process, it was worth a try.

Joe pushed open the door to Rosie's and glanced around the noisy café. There was a booth close to the door, and he quickly claimed it.

"Hey, Joe," someone called.

Joe looked around and spotted Karl DeLange, a shorter, older man sitting at a table a few feet away with some other men. "Hey, yourself, Karl. How's that horse working out for you?"

"Great. You did good with that little mare. I only hope I can keep it up with her," he replied.

"You won't be able to," joked one of his table-mates. Joe recognized him as an equipment dealer. "You'll never have the way with women that Joe has."

General laughter followed that. Joe smiled and turned just as Rebecca opened the door. She glanced carefully around, and Joe was aware of a hush. People glanced at her, checking out the stranger in town.

She spotted Joe, smiled a grateful smile and slowly walked over. Joe got up as she sat down. "Hi, there," he said.

"What did I say, Karl?" the equipment dealer said loudly. "That Joe moves faster than his own horses."

Joe glanced at Rebecca, hoping she hadn't heard. She was looking at the menu, and he couldn't read her expression.

He pulled out a menu and gave it a cursory glance. He knew what he wanted, but it gave him something to do.

"Coffee?" The waitress held out a pot of coffee, and Joe looked across at Rebecca who politely declined.

"Sure," Joe said. He held out his cup and looked directly into the hard brown eyes of Kristine. She poured him a cup, frowning at him all the while.

"You've been a busy man, Joe." Her voice said one thing, but Joe knew she was alluding to Rebecca, and he didn't like it. Kristine had no claims on his time or his attention.

"Working on the ranch has kept me busy, yes," he said quietly.

"Among other things," Kristine said with a cold smirk, glancing at Rebecca.

"I wouldn't mind a cup of tea, when you have time," Rebecca quietly asked.

Kristine glanced at Rebecca with a forced smile. "Sure. I'll get it." She turned and left.

Joe sat back, frustrated with the tension Kristine had created. He didn't know what to say to Rebecca. She looked across the table at him, one corner of her mouth turned up in a smile.

"Was she the woman I saw you with at the bank the first day you came?"

"She wasn't with me," Joe replied, putting heavy emphasis on the word *with.*

Rebecca nodded, smiling. "Good."

Joe took encouragement from her light comment and leaned forward. "I'm glad you came," he said simply, wanting to establish a connection with her, to start somewhere. He felt an urge to reach across the table and take her hand, but stopped himself. Play it cool, Brewer. What's come over you?

Kristine bustled up with a teacup and a small pot and set them carefully in front of Rebecca. She pulled a pen and a pad out of the pocket of her apron. "Have you decided what you want?"

"A cheeseburger and fries, please," Rebecca said.

Joe blinked in surprise. Rebecca caught his incredulous look. "What?" she said with a light laugh.

"Nothing. I'm just…" He let the sentence drift off, aware of Kristine watching them.

"Thinking I would order a salad?"

"Yeah. I guess." He grinned at her. "I'll have the same," he said to Kristine.

Kristine took the menus, gave Joe one last pleading

look, which he ignored, then with a flip of her dark hair, strode away.

Joe leaned his elbows on the table, his hands clasped in front of him as he racked his mind to find something witty or pleasant to say—anything to remove the atmosphere Kristine had left behind.

"Hey, Joe," a voice called in greeting, and Joe looked up, stifling a sigh. It was Merle, and old high school buddy.

"How's the new shop coming along?" Joe asked as Merle stopped at the table, holding his hat and his counter check.

"Good." Merle nodded briefly at Rebecca. "Ma'am."

"Merle, this is Rebecca Stevenson. She's working at the bank. Taking Karen's place while she's having her baby." Joe tilted his head toward Merle. "Rebecca, this is Merle. He just started up a welding shop in the industrial park on the edge of town."

Merle held out a grease-stained hand, and Rebecca took it quickly, her mouth curved in a polite smile. Merle leaned against the booth, settling in for a nice long chat, and Joe groaned. This was not how he had envisioned his time with Rebecca.

Merle's talk meandered over interest rates, the weather, the price of steel and how hard it was to find good help. "You know all about that, eh, Joe?"

Joe nodded, trying to find a way to politely ask him to leave. When their food arrived, he thought Merle might take the hint.

Instead Merle turned his hat in his hands, standing aside momentarily while Kristine served Joe and Rebecca their meal. As Kristine set Joe's food in front of him, her hands lingered on the plate. She tried to catch his eye.

Joe felt surrounded by his past. While he watched, Rebecca folded her hands in her lap and looked down. Joe wondered if she was praying.

He gave Kristine a curt nod, and she left.

Merle chatted on. Joe's food sat in front of him, its mouthwatering fragrance making his stomach rumble. He had missed breakfast this morning.

Finally he looked at Merle. "You know, Merle, I'm hungry and I'd like to say a blessing, if you don't mind."

Merle looked taken aback. "No. Sorry. Go ahead." But he still didn't move.

Joe took a breath, glanced quickly at Rebecca, who looked at him, her eyes twinkling. "And I'd like to visit with Miss Stevenson. Alone."

There. He had said it, and Rebecca was still smiling. Merle's face took on a knowing look. "Of course, Joe. Sorry." He winked broadly, and with a quick nod at Rebecca, sauntered away.

Joe bent his head, struggled to concentrate on his prayer, apologizing to the Lord at the same time. He waited a moment, then looked up to see Rebecca, one hand over her mouth as if stifling laughter.

"What's so funny?"

"I'm sorry, Joe. It just looked humorous seeing

you practically drooling over your food while your friend kept going on. Why didn't you just start eating?"

Joe pulled the ketchup toward him, frowning. "I like to pray before my meal."

"It's a good habit," she conceded.

"It's more than a habit, Rebecca." He squeezed a generous amount of ketchup on his plate and set the bottle down. "I'm thankful for everything I have. And praying before a meal is a reminder that everything I have comes from God."

Rebecca looked at him, delicately nibbling a fry. "You have a very basic faith, don't you?"

"I have a very simple faith. I've not been a Christian that long." Joe took a bit of his burger, then wiped his mouth. "But you're lucky."

Rebecca frowned. "Why do you say that?"

"The other day you told me how you were raised, to believe. How your whole family goes to church." He looked at his food, toying with a sprig of parsley. "There's no one in my extended family who understands. Old friends think I'm crazy, and that this will pass. But I know it won't. I need God. I'm lucky I've got the people in the church here. They've been great."

He looked at Rebecca, who was watching him, her head tilted, her slightly angled eyes softened by the smile on her face. "I'm not the lucky one, Joe. You are," she said quietly.

He wanted to ask her more, but she looked quickly away. "You must know everybody in Wakely."

"Hard not to. The population in a place like this doesn't change much. About half the kids I went to school with stuck around, taking over their parents' land or finding work in town."

"Speaking of taking over a parent's place…" Rebecca dipped a fry in ketchup and took a dainty bite. "The paperwork is just about done on the loan transfer. We should have final approval by the end of the week."

Joe nodded. He didn't want to talk about the loan or think about the finality of it. He preferred to live in the nebulous present—caught between what he had to do and what he wanted.

Rebecca glanced around the café. "Wakely is a neat little town."

"It has its negatives and positives. Like most places." Joe finished his burger and wiped his fingers. "You always live in Calgary?"

Rebecca nodded, taking another delicate bite of her burger. She did everything in that same well-mannered way, thought Joe. Even eating a big sloppy cheeseburger. She dabbed the corner of her mouth. "Dad has his own business based out of Calgary. We fly down to Denver once in awhile. He has a partner that works out of there. And Los Angeles."

"Wow. You must have seen a lot of different places."

Rebecca shrugged. "A hotel is a hotel whether it's

in Switzerland or L.A.'' She smiled at him. ''Lest you think I'm sounding like a poor little rich girl, I know I've had a good life. I have parents who love me and a sister who is somewhat protective, but caring. I just don't get the kick out of traveling that my parents do. I like being at home.''

''Home being your parents' place in Calgary. The place that's bigger than Jenna's.''

''It's still just a house, Joe. Doesn't matter how you fancy it up. It's just rooms and space. It's the people who live in it that make a house a home, regardless of its size.''

Easy for her to say, he thought, remembering too well what Jenna's place looked like. But she sounded melancholy. ''So what is the perfect home for you?'' he asked, pushing his plate aside, folding his arms on the table between them.

Rebecca glanced up quickly. ''Anyplace where I can be with someone who cares about me, who I care about, too.''

Joe felt his heart lift at her words. He hardly dared think that material possessions didn't matter to her, hardly dared think that he might have the inkling of a chance with her. She had come today, he reminded himself. Without a lot of coercion. Would she be willing to try again? ''I was wondering if you wanted to come on a picnic this weekend,'' he asked before he changed his mind.

Rebecca held his steady gaze, her expression softening. ''I'd like that.''

"That's great," he replied, sitting a little straighter. "A bunch of the youth group are using a couple of my horses. They're heading out early, and I want to make sure they're all okay before I come and get you. I thought we could head up around ten."

"You don't have to come and get me," she said quickly. "I'll meet you at your place. Sounds like you'll be busy."

Joe frowned. "I don't mind picking you up."

"No, that's fine. I can meet you at your place at ten. We'll have more time that way."

That was true enough. Besides, she seemed quite adamant about driving herself. Independent. He decided to humor her. "Okay. I don't like it, but okay."

"I'm a woman of the nineties, Joe. We don't need to be coddled."

"I don't see you as the coddling type, anyhow."

Rebecca leaned forward. "Really, Joe? How do you see me?"

He frowned. "I think you're an independent person. I sensed that from the first…" His voice drifted off as he remembered their first meeting.

"Joe." Rebecca reached across the table, her hand resting lightly on his. "I'm still sorry about snapping at you the way I did that day." She bit her lip, lifted her shoulder in a shrug. "I get overly sensitive about my leg."

Joe turned his hand to hold hers, his warm, hers cool. "That's okay," he said quietly, "I tend to get a little over-helpful. I imagine you've had enough of that.''

"I have." Rebecca laughed shortly. "That's half the reason I came here. To get away from my over-helpful mother. I was getting tired of being a daughter who limped. I just wanted to be her daughter."

Joe held her hand lightly, still surprised at her spontaneous touch, enjoying the slight contact. "It must have been hard for you."

"It was. Is. I still struggle with it. When I came into the café, it was there again. The second looks, the frowns. I've stopped being a person. I'm now a limp attached to a woman." Rebecca tried to pull her hand away, but Joe, surprised at his own audacity, held on, sensing that she was withdrawing in another way.

"Actually I think people were looking at a beautiful stranger. Quite a devastating combination in a town the size of Wakely." Joe rubbed his thumb along the side of her hand, marveling at her slender fingers, delicate against his rough palm.

Rebecca's fingers tightened against his, her gaze holding his, a smile curving her lips. "Thanks, Joe," she said quietly. The moment stretched, lengthened, as they sat, isolated, alone, unaware of the noise and crowd around them.

"Will there be anything else?" Kristine's harsh voice shattered the mood. Rebecca pulled her hand away, and Joe straightened.

"I think we're okay." Joe glanced at Kristine's narrowed eyes. "Thanks."

Kristine laid a check on the table and walked away. Joe took it, leaned sideways and pulled his wallet out of his pants pocket.

Rebecca reached for her purse at the same time.

"I'll get this," Joe said quickly.

"I can pay for my share."

"I know that," Joe said. "But you're not the only one who wants to be independent."

"And what do you think people will say when they find out that you've been taking your banker to lunch?" Rebecca teased.

Joe glanced at her, surprised at her quick humor. He grinned as he pulled a few bills out of his wallet and dropped them on the table. "I think the guys will be jealous."

Rebecca laughed. Joe slipped out of the booth, waiting for her, and they walked out of the café together.

"So I'll see you Saturday?" Joe asked as they stopped at the door to the bank.

"I'll be there at ten."

Joe nodded, his thumbs strung in his belt loops. "I'll be waiting."

Rebecca tossed him one last smile and pulled open the door to the bank. As it fell shut behind her, Joe blew out his breath. He turned, fully aware that he was grinning a foolish grin. He didn't care.

Thank you, Lord, he exulted, sauntering down the sidewalk to his truck.

"I think we're finally seeing some improvement." Heather smiled carefully at Rebecca, watching as she clung to the handrail of the treadmill.

Rebecca nodded. She was too tired to answer. She was thankful Heather could see a change, but for Rebecca it still involved a lot of hard work and pain. She had stopped praying, figuring she would concentrate on the work part of the work-and-pray equation.

"Do you want to quit now?" Heather asked, watching Rebecca.

"Should I?" Rebecca asked, taking a shaky breath.

"That's up to you. As far as I can see you're still looking pretty good. I'd go another five minutes. Not much more."

Rebecca's leg was tired and starting to ache. She felt like quitting, but she kept thinking of her date with Joe this weekend. She kept thinking of the women who surrounded him like bees around a flower.

More disturbing was the vision that stayed stubbornly in her mind. Stephanie running to Joe, the woman at the restaurant walking away. Both women whole and sound and normal.

She pushed on.

Chapter Eleven

Rebecca savored her last bite of apple pie, carefully wiping a few flaky crumbs from her mouth. "That was delicious," she said, setting down the paper napkin.

"I usually have to do some creative begging to get apple pie," Joe said, wiping his mouth, "but today I think I outdid myself." He sent her a sidelong glance that she could only describe as mischievous, and Rebecca couldn't help the answering beat of her heart.

She looked away, busying herself with cleaning up the plates and cups they had used. She had to smile at the differences between the setting of this week's date compared to last week's.

Instead of a string quartet, the gentle warbling of sparrows contrasted with the sharp caw of crows in the trees above them. The wind sighed through the boughs of the pine trees, instead of the hushed sound of people talking. Instead of cut flowers floating in a crystal bowl, wild crocuses lay scattered on the blanket between them. A bright sun was softened by the grove of trees Joe had chosen for the picnic. Her escort of today wore blue jeans and a slightly wrinkled white T-shirt. She couldn't imagine him in the suit and tie that Dale had favored.

"And what is going on behind those bright blue eyes right about now?" asked Joe with a grin as he took the dirty plates and glasses from her and set them in the cooler.

She could have said something evasive but wondered what he would do if she told the truth. "I'm just comparing this supper with last week's."

"And what's the verdict on today?" he asked, closing the cooler.

Rebecca tilted her head, studying him. He sat with his legs bent at the knees, his wrists resting on them, much as he had the first time she saw him. But a light frown marred the smooth line of his forehead. One corner of his mouth was pulled down, as if in displeasure. She felt a curiously feminine wave of pleasure. He was jealous. "I think I like this better," she said, deciding to let him off the hook.

"I'm glad about that," he said quietly. Joe got up, carried the cooler to the truck and set it in the back. He came back and stopped beside her.

Rebecca had to shade her eyes as she looked at him, towering above her. He reached down, and she put her hand in his without questioning. With a gentle tug, he pulled her to her feet. "You up for a short walk?"

"I'd like that."

"I want to show you something," said Joe, standing close to her.

He turned and led her down a well-worn trail. She speculated on how many other women he had brought here, how many others had been swept away by his good looks and gentle charm.

Probably more than I would want to count, she thought, wondering why she was allowing herself to be added to the number.

They walked through the quiet forest, branches hanging over the narrow trail, the aspen trees still showing the tender green of spring.

Joe kept the pace slow, one hand in his pocket, the other holding hers lightly.

The cool of the morning hung in the trees. The air was fresh, clean, and Rebecca deeply inhaled the tangy scent of new buds mingling with the moldering smell of decaying leaves underfoot.

"It's so quiet here," she said as they walked along.

"I used to drive the truck up to this place, radio on full tilt, singing along to some forgettable rock and roll song," Joe replied. "Then I'd turn off the radio and just let the quiet press in on me."

"Did you come here often?"

"As often as I could sneak away."

"And how many women did you bring up here?" Rebecca tried to keep her tone light, tried to convey a knowledge of who he was and his appeal to the various women he met.

Joe stopped, turning to her with a gentle smile. "I brought an old girlfriend, Gail, here once, when we were going out. But that was a long time ago." He held her hand a little tighter, his gaze intent. "I've never brought anyone here since then."

Rebecca couldn't look away and didn't want to. She wasn't sure if she completely understood what he meant, and she didn't know why it suddenly bothered her to think of him with a woman named Gail.

He started walking again.

Rebecca glanced at him, but he was looking ahead. His wavy hair was a little windblown, his mouth relaxed, his eyes on the path they walked on. She didn't need to watch as closely as he did, she thought, clutching his arm a little tighter. He was leading her. He would make sure she didn't stumble, and she trusted that he would take care of her.

"We're just about there," Joe said softly, glancing at her. She nodded, looking away.

Then the trees thinned and suddenly they stood on the edge of the world.

At least that's how it looked to Rebecca. Below her feet the land fell away on all sides, flowing down to the plains on one side, to the creek that spooled like a silver ribbon below them.

On the other side, the mountains rose up, green giving way to bare hard rock and above that snow-encrusted peaks.

"You made him ruler over the works of Your hands. You put everything under his feet." The words slipped out before Rebecca was aware she said them.

She pulled away from Joe, walking over to a large pine tree, its boughs making shade in the warmth of the afternoon sun. "This is absolutely incredible." Rebecca leaned against the pine tree, the bark warmed by the sun. She slowly lowered herself till she was sitting, drew her knees close to her and wrapped her arms around them.

Joe dropped beside her and plucked a blade of dried grass. He turned his head, his chin resting on his shoulder, his brown eyes glinting at her. "Where's that quote from?" he asked quietly.

Rebecca let herself be drawn into his gaze, allowed herself a brief moment of awareness to acknowledge his attraction for her. "Psalm eight, I think. Don't ask me which verse."

"How do you remember that?" he asked, surprise in his voice.

"In junior high, we had to learn a psalm every week. Or part of it if the psalm was especially long. They slip out every now and then. Trouble with photographic memory." Rebecca let her gaze drift over the valley, unable to take in the sweep and grandeur of the landscape in one pass. "I can't believe you don't come up here every day," she said with a laugh. "How could you ever get enough of this view?"

"I used to come up a lot when I was a kid. Whenever I wanted to get away from the work on the ranch or if I had to check out the cows on the lease." Joe lay back, his arms crossed behind his head, his booted feet crossed at the ankle. "It is nice, isn't it?"

"Nice?" Rebecca leaned forward as if to get closer to the empty space that yawned below her, the absolute majesty of it. "How can you size this all up with that tiny little word?"

Joe laughed. "I guess nice is pretty lame. I never was great with words. But it's funny how that goes with something you have known since your youth. It becomes a part of you that you can't seem to separate, that you don't even know how to explain to someone else."

Rebecca had the feeling he was alluding to more than just the view, and she wasn't so sure she wanted to go there.

Instead she glanced at Joe, so close beside her, his hair falling across his forehead.

At that moment he looked at her and smiled, working the grass to the other side of his mouth. "You are looking like a banker."

"That's good," she said. "I practice my banker face every day in front of the mirror. Can't afford to slip up."

Joe hitched himself up, leaning his head on one hand, his other hand pulling the grass out of his mouth as he grinned. "I imagine you can't afford to let your clients know that any minute you are about to change their life forever."

Rebecca felt a small jolt at his words, wondering

if he was talking about his family. He had mentioned it only briefly, but she felt a sudden need to know his feelings on the subject. "Does that bother you, this business with your brother and the ranch?" She clasped her legs a little tighter, ignoring the twinge in her hip, waiting for his answer.

Joe traced the outline of a rock imbedded in the ground, as if trying to draw out the words he wanted. "Yes. I was angry with my father for a long time for giving so much to Lane. It would have worked out better if Dad had willed the place to me and got me to pay Lane out. Lane would have had his money, at least at first, and I would have had a ranch. But Lane was his favorite, and I was a high school dropout."

"Why did you drop out of school?"

Joe sighed and looked at Rebecca, his mouth quirked in a wry grin. "I should get you to talk to Lorna McLure."

Rebecca frowned.

"Old junior high school teacher. She could give you chapter and verse, none of it biblical." Joe let the grass drift across the rock as he frowned. "She could tell you about missed classes and endless homework. Ever since I was old enough to help, Dad was pulling me out to help with branding, shipping calves, haying and all the other stuff that comes with working on a ranch. I missed so much school, and dear Lorna tried to help me keep up. But I got sick of working myself ragged trying to keep up with the ranch and my schoolwork and never satisfying the other teachers or my father. I got sick of failing tests because I missed them, sick of seeing those low numbers on my report card. I got sick of listening to my father yelling at me because I didn't move fast enough." Joe squinted at the sky and shrugged. "So I quit both and started working for a trucking company. As soon as I could, I got my class one license and started driving. I don't think my father ever forgave me."

Rebecca held her legs tighter, unable to look away from him, trying to imagine a young boy struggling with school and a workload that was far beyond his capabilities. "You don't sound bitter about it."

Joe frowned and turned to Rebecca, his expression serious. "I had my moments. Still do. Hating my father took up a lot of time and energy. But thankfully, I was able to see him in the hospital as he was dying. He didn't ask me for forgiveness. We didn't have a big reconciliation scene. He was so out of it he didn't even recognize Lane or me." Joe stopped and looked away, shaking his head. "It was easier to forgive him then. By that time I had become a Christian. I had learned that God forgave me so much more, it would be petty if I couldn't forgive my own dying father. Lane was a little harder."

Rebecca's heart began a slow heavy beat. Forgiveness. Easy to accept, so hard to give. "You make it sound so effortless," she said softly, unable to look away from him, as if by holding his gaze, she could discover how he had done it.

"It wasn't. I still struggle with it. When I made out

that five-year plan, it was as if I was back to where I was before I was a Christian.'' He slowly sat up, pulling himself closer to her. ''I had to forgive my father and my brother all over again. But I don't do it on my own strength, Rebecca.''

She couldn't look away, couldn't stop the heaviness in her heart. ''Where do you start with it all?''

''By letting go of anger. By not letting it determine what you're going to do.'' He laughed. ''I've never been real good at having someone or something dictate my actions. My lack of forgiveness was taking over my life, and I resented that.''

Rebecca laid her head on her knees as an unexpected sorrow engulfed her. Let go. He made it sound so easy. She still struggled with anger against a man she no longer cared for, against an accident that had only left her with a limp against the complete reversal of her life. She swallowed hard and drew in a trembling breath. She wouldn't cry in front of Joe.

''I wish I could quote you something,'' he continued, his soft voice compelling, comforting. He stopped stroking her back, his hand resting on her neck, the other covering her hands. ''I wish I could remember some verse that would give you comfort,'' he whispered, laying his head close to hers.

''I know lots of them,'' she said, swallowing the tightness in her throat at his tenderness and concern. She drew in a shaky breath and looked across the valley to the mountains.

''Tell me one,'' he encouraged.

Rebecca closed her eyes as she drew into her past, her memory. "It is God who arms me with strength and makes my way perfect. He makes my feet like the feet of a deer. He enables me to stand on the heights." Rebecca whispered the words.

"And here you are." Joe cupped her face, turning it toward him. "Up on the heights."

Rebecca's laugh was without humor. "But you brought me here."

Joe's fingers traced her features, his calluses rough on her skin. His soft brown eyes followed his fingers as they traveled over her face. "I think God brought you here, Rebecca," he said quietly as he bent and touched his lips to hers.

Rebecca felt a sob gather in her throat, and as it gathered strength she reached out and caught him, wanting to draw from his strength, his faith.

He held her close, rocking gently back and forth. "You know so much, Rebecca," he murmured against her hair. "You know what to do. Think with your heart, not your head this time."

His words flowed over her. His arms held her, and she dared think that she had found exactly what she had been seeking since she first learned about God.

They stayed thus, each holding, each hardly daring to think that in this moment seeking had become finding.

Joe was the first to pull away. Once again, he raised Rebecca's chin. "Are you okay?" he asked, tenderness in his voice.

Rebecca smiled tremulously, bemused by his consideration. "How did you get to be such a nice guy, Joe Brewer?"

Joe quirked his mouth in a wry grin. "I only wish I was. I grumble and complain and lose my temper."

"I can't imagine that."

He let his hand rest on her cheek, cupping it gently, his expression suddenly serious. His rough fingers feathered her cheek, and his eyes seemed to delve into her. "I'm just an ordinary guy, Rebecca. I don't have a lot." He stopped, as if unable to say more.

Rebecca turned her mouth to press a kiss against his palm, her hand holding his tightly against her cheek. She knew what he was saying, and she didn't want him to continue. "You have more than I do, Joe," she said quietly. "You have a faith that I envy, a relationship with God that I haven't had for a while now. I see a man who truly loves God. I haven't had that love for a while now."

"Do you think you can't get it back?" Joe's quiet question struck deep into her.

"I don't know." She sat up, letting his hand drop, but he twined his fingers through hers as if in encouragement. "God has felt distant to me ever since I woke up in the hospital, and it's like I can't generate the emotions I once had."

"But you go to church."

Rebecca shrugged. "I know. And I sometimes feel like a hypocrite." She rubbed her forehead with a finger, as if trying to draw out the right answers. "I

keep going through the motions, hoping that somehow the spark, that first love will come back. But my
life flows on, the same yet so different. Nothing
changes, and yet everything has." She looked at Joe,
frowning. "Does this make any sense to you?"

"Sort of." Joe sat back against the pine tree, cross-
legged, as he toyed with her fingers, his eyes following the movements of his hand. Then he looked at
the valley below them. "When I said the view was
nice, you said the word was too small. Maybe it is.
But I've seen this place so many times I probably
take it for granted. It doesn't generate this huge emotion in me, just a sense of rightness, of belonging."
He pulled Rebecca close to his side.

So easily she laid her head against the warmth of
his chest. It felt so natural, so right, to fit herself
against him, to let his arms come around her and hold
her close.

"You see the valley in one huge, overwhelming
swoop," he continued, "I see smaller things. There's
a tree farther down that splits into three. Up the valley
the river tumbles down some rocks, creating the most
incredible waterfall. I've seen this place through different seasons. I've been caught up here in a snowstorm. I've swatted mosquitoes on this ridge. I've
seen the sun color it gold and I've seen it through a
blinding snowstorm." He stroked the top of her head
with his chin, his voice a soft rumble under her cheek.
"I don't see the same valley you do because I have
different experiences. I don't have the same emotional

response. Instead it's much more a part of me. In my mind I can see it a hundred different ways, and each of them has its own beauty. I think it's the same way with your faith and mine. I still have that emotional response to God. I still remember vividly the emotions I felt when I found out that my mistakes, my anger, my past were forgiven. You've known it all your life. That gives you a richness and depth that you can draw on. A depth that I don't have."

Rebecca listened, a melancholy drifting over her at his words. "You make it sound very straightforward."

"And you seem to insist on making it harder than it is." He pressed a kiss to her head, gave her a quick hug. "I feel funny giving you spiritual advice, but like I said before, I think you're trying too hard."

Rebecca sighed lightly. "I suppose." She lifted her head, smiling at him. "And I think you're a pretty wonderful person, Joe Brewer." She reached up to trace the fine line of his mouth, the darkness of his eyebrows.

He looked at her and was just about to kiss her again when the honking of a horn shattered the stillness. Joe frowned, glancing over his shoulder. "That sounds like my truck."

Rebecca drew away as he got up. "How do you know?"

Joe winked at her. "I know my master's voice. I'll be right back."

Rebecca got up slowly, brushing bits of leaves off

her jeans. She stretched out her leg, flexing some muscles, and looked across the valley again, thinking about Joe's analogy. "He should have been a preacher," she murmured with a grin, trying to imagine him on a pulpit. It didn't work. That unruly hair made her want to smooth it out, and those flashing brown eyes and that mischievous dimple would be too distracting for any female member of the congregation.

She heard Joe's voice, then another person's, harsh and sharp. Then the truck motor started up. Curious, she walked carefully down the path, brushing overhanging branches out of her face.

She came to the clearing in time to see the brake lights of Joe's pickup flash as it slowed then turned and headed down the hill. Joe stood in the clearing, holding a horse's reins, talking quietly to the animal, his hand stroking its neck.

He turned as Rebecca came near. "Hi, there." He continued stroking the horse. "One of the girls from the youth group had an accident with this horse. The leader walked her and the horse over here, hoping to meet up with me. He's taking her to the hospital right now."

"What happened?" Rebecca walked a wide circle around Joe and the horse, watching it warily.

"They think she broke her nose. I told them to leave the horse here and take the truck. I said we'd ride Ben back."

"How will we do that?" she asked, her heart beginning to pound as she tried to understand what he was saying.

"We'll ride him double. He's a big enough horse. I'll take the saddle off, and you can ride in front of me." Joe shot her a puzzled glance, then realization dawned. "Oh, Rebecca, I'm sorry." Joe ran a hand through his hair and blew out his breath in a sigh. "I don't know how I forgot."

Rebecca swallowed a knot of fear. "I can't do that, Joe. I'd sooner walk back."

"It's too far for you, Rebecca," he said softly.

She looked away, knowing he was right. Any other woman could walk all the way, but not her. And any other woman wouldn't be afraid to ride the horse.

"Why didn't you call me? I could have ridden back with whoever it was. In the truck." Her fear rose along with her anger that he had put her in this predicament.

"He was in a hurry. The poor girl was bleeding all over the place, and I truly didn't think much of it until now." He let the reins drop and walked over to her. "It will be okay, Rebecca. I'll be behind you. He's a quiet horse."

"Then how did that girl break her nose?"

"She didn't know what she was doing, and the horse didn't know what she wanted. It was inexperience, that's all." Joe stroked her shoulders with his palms, as if reassuring her, his voice soothing. "I know this horse. I know what I'm doing. You'll have to trust me, Rebecca."

She sighed, feeling pushed into a corner with no escape. "I don't like this, Joe."

"I didn't set this up. I didn't even think about your fear of horses. I'm sorry, believe me." He bent his head to catch her eye, his voice pleading.

She looked at him. He was frowning, his expression one of concern.

"Please trust me?"

And at that moment, with his hands resting on her shoulders, his eyes holding hers, she knew she could.

"Okay," she said in resignation. "But no fancy stuff."

Joe's grin lit up his face. "You can't do much fancy with two people on a horse."

She smiled tremulously, then, biting her lip, looked at the horse.

Joe is going to be behind me, she reminded herself. Joe said he would take care of me. She clutched Joe's hand for support and walked slowly to the animal, stifling an automatic clutch of fear at its size.

"I'll get up first and then help you on, okay?"

Rebecca nodded, swallowing, her eyes fixed firmly on the horse. Joe let go of her hand and walked ahead of her. He tugged on a strap and loosened a buckle and then, in one easy motion, pulled the saddle and blanket off. Then he vaulted easily onto the back of the horse.

"Come on over, Rebecca," he said, reaching down to catch the reins.

Rebecca pulled in a deep breath and, keeping her eyes on Joe, did as he said.

"Just come up beside Ben and turn your back to him," he instructed, his voice quiet, almost hushed.

Rebecca flinched as the horse tossed its head at her approach. She stopped. She couldn't seem to move. She tried to reason her way past the sense of foreboding, tried to convince herself that nothing would go wrong, that it was just an animal. But all her practical arguments couldn't seem to get past the knot of fear in her throat.

"Don't look at the horse, Rebecca," Joe instructed. "Just look at me."

Rebecca swallowed, pressed a trembling hand against her beating heart and turned her gaze to Joe. He smiled, one hand reaching out to her.

"That's good," he said. "Just walk toward me."

Still looking at Joe, Rebecca took a few steps and then she was beside this large, warm animal. Close enough to smell the distinct tang of horse, close enough that she could feel the heat radiating off its body.

"Okay, now turn around. When I pull you up, you lift one leg over Ben's neck, okay?"

Rebecca nodded and then, before she had even completed the turn, she was lifted in strong hands. Her leg automatically went over, and she sat snugly in front of Joe. One arm held her close, the other held the reins.

"You okay?" His voice was a soft rumble in her

ear. Rebecca nodded, trying not to notice how far away the ground looked. The horse shook its head once more.

"You sure this horse is okay with both of us on him?" Rebecca didn't quite know what to do with her hands, so she clutched Joe's arm.

"I'm positive. Ben is my calmest horse."

"I wonder if the girl with the bloody nose would agree with that," Rebecca said, stiffening as Ben took a quick step sideways.

"Haven't you ever hit your head on something or stubbed your toe?"

Rebecca frowned. "Yes, but what has that to do with—"

"It was the same thing. She leaned forward just as Ben lifted his head. Accident. Horses aren't out to get you, they don't have a personal vendetta with humans because we ride them." Joe clucked to the horse, and he turned. Another sound from Joe, and Ben began walking slowly down the trail toward home.

Rebecca tried not to tense up with each sway of the horse, with each muffled thud of hooves on the ground.

"Relax, Rebecca," Joe murmured in her ear, his strong arm tightening around her waist. "I've got you. I won't let you go."

Rebecca closed her eyes and leaned back against his broad chest, allowing his arms to hold her, his strength and warmth to surround her. The movements of the horse were calm, unhurried, and with Joe's arm around her, she began to relax.

After a few minutes, when nothing had happened, she opened her eyes. The trail they had driven up in the truck had a different look from the back of a horse. The scenery drifted leisurely past, allowing her a chance to see with more depth and clarity what she had only glimpsed through the windows of Joe's truck.

"How are you doing?" Joe asked quietly, his mouth beside her ear.

"I'm fine. Thanks." And she was.

Joe rubbed his chin slowly along Rebecca's hair, gently inhaling the delicate scent of her perfume mingled with shampoo. In his arms she felt small, fragile, though he knew better. She felt so good nestled against him, he had to resist the urge to hold her even closer. "You sure you're okay?" he asked, needing to know.

She nodded, her hands holding his arm. "I'm fine, Joe, really. This horse seems pretty quiet."

"Ben is fairly bulletproof. He used to be a pickup horse for a rodeo."

"What's that?" Rebecca tilted her head to look at him.

Joe couldn't resist dropping a light kiss on her cheek. She turned and smiled at him. "Are you avoiding my question?"

"No," he said with a smile. "Getting distracted."

"So what is a pickup horse?"

"A pickup guy is the man who helps cowboys off the horses during the saddle bronc and the bareback events in the rodeo. When the horn for the eight-second mark goes off, the pickup man comes alongside the bucking horse and the cowboy jumps off the bronc onto the pickup horse, or grabs hold of the rider and pulls himself over."

"Sounds dangerous." Rebecca laid her head against Joe's chest.

"It is. And you need a very calm and dependable horse for that. That's my Ben."

Ben flicked one ear at the sound of his name. "You're a good horse, Ben. I'm glad you're behaving so gentlemanly for Rebecca," Joe said, patting Ben's neck in acknowledgment.

"You talk to your horses a lot?"

"Yes, I do. I'm a big mush when it comes to these animals. Most of my horses have such a good heart and would do anything for me."

"Do you use your horses around the ranch?"

"Yup. Most of the horses have to earn their keep one way or the other. Mack is good for moving cows, and I use Ben for tight work. Cutting out animals that need a shot, separating calves, that kind of thing."

Rebecca was quiet for awhile, seemingly content to just ride. She felt more pliable, less uptight than she had in the beginning. At first Joe had felt terrible at how events had transpired, but with her sitting securely against him, her arms pressed against his, her head resting against his shoulder, he knew that things had worked out exactly as they should.

He prayed that this ride would help her overcome her fear of horses. But even more, he prayed it would cement their relationship. Because with each step of Ben's feet he knew beyond a doubt that he was falling in love with her. She was on his mind constantly. He felt a need to be with her that he had never felt with any other woman. It was as if she was the part of his life he missed.

The trail opened from woods to fields. Too soon they reached the first gate in the fences that marked off his property from the leased land on the hills.

He dismounted and opened the gate. Rebecca held onto Ben's mane as he led the horse through, but she looked relaxed and smiled at him when he walked to mount up.

"The countryside has a different look when you're on a horse, doesn't it?" she asked as he settled behind her once again. "You're so high up."

"Ben's a bigger animal than a lot of horses, but sure, sitting on a horse gives you a different outlook. I like exploring on horseback better than on foot."

They chatted as Ben plodded along. Inconsequential things, the give and take of two people slowly finding their way around each other. Rebecca asked him about ranching, and he asked her about growing up in the city. Both avoided talking about banking and loans.

Too soon the corrals and fences of Joe's yard came

into view. Joe regretted the moment when they would come to the yard and the magic of the afternoon would be replaced by the mundane reality of chores and trying to figure out what he was going to make for supper. He wondered if he dared ask her to stay.

They went through the open gate to the hitching post, and Joe dismounted. He looped Ben's reins over the post then reached for Rebecca.

With a smile, she held out her arms and easily slid off the horse. And then it seemed perfectly natural to press her close, to capture her mouth with his, to let one hand drift through her silky hair, tangling his fingers in it.

She returned his kiss, her hands clutching his back, and Joe was taken up in the wonder of it all.

Slowly he drew away, his hand still holding her head, his arm still wrapped around her waist. He laid his forehead against hers as he drew in a contented sigh. "You are a very precious person, Rebecca Stevenson," he said softly.

She murmured a soft protest, which he stilled with another quick kiss.

"I want to spend more time with you. I want to get to know you better." He drew back to look into her eyes, to read her emotions.

Her answering smile warmed and encouraged him. "When can I see you again?" he asked. "Are you busy after church tomorrow?"

She shook her head. "Do you want to try to get

me on the back of a horse again?'' she asked with a hint of laughter in her voice.

"Did you mind?'' He stroked her hair from her face, his eyes watching his hands as if they were separate from him, daring to touch this woman, daring to take such liberties.

"No,'' she said softly, her arms still around him. "I wish I could tell you what you have given me today.'' She held his gaze, her blue eyes intent. "You're a pretty wonderful person yourself, Joe Brewer.''

He felt his heart lift. "I'm glad you enjoyed yourself,'' he replied, his heart full. "I really have to thank the Lord for today.''

"Yes,'' she replied, looking past him at the mountains beyond. "I do, too.''

And those three words, more than anything else, gave him hope and peace.

"I hate to put an end to this, but I should go,'' Rebecca said.

Joe nodded, tucked her arm in his and walked her to her truck. "Can I pick you up for church tomorrow?''

Rebecca dropped her hand and took a step back. "It's so far out of the way....''

Joe was puzzled at her sudden change. "No, it isn't. Church is in town, and Troy and Jenna don't live that far out of town.''

"I'll let you know, okay?'' She bit her lip, avoiding his gaze.

Joe frowned. "Okay," he said. "Do you still want to come over after church?"

"Oh, yes." Rebecca's gaze flew to his, and her hands reached out to him. "Yes, I do."

He was reassured, and his shoulders relaxed. "Well, then, I'll see you tomorrow in church."

She smiled and nodded. "I'll see you then, Joe." She let go of his hands. Joe reached past her to open her door, and she smiled at him once more as she got in.

"Drive carefully," he said softly before he pushed the door shut.

Rebecca started the truck, buckled up and with another brilliant smile, put the truck in gear and left.

Joe felt as if his heart was going to burst. It seemed inconceivable. He hardly dared think of where their relationship would go.

"One day at a time," Joe said to himself as Rebecca turned onto the road. "One day at a time."

Chapter Twelve

Rebecca pulled into the driveway and parked beside her sister's car. Jenna had been gone when Rebecca left this morning.

Rebecca wished she could stop the foolish pounding of her heart at the thought of facing her sister.

Grow up, Becks, she chided herself. You're old enough to be living on your own, and you're still scared to face your sister and tell her where you've been.

Are you ashamed of Joe?

Rebecca bit her lip. She knew she wasn't. But she also knew that right now she didn't want to listen to her sister ruin her perfect day by going on about the unsuitability of Joe Brewer.

And go on she would. Rebecca knew from experience that once Jenna had a hold of something, she hung onto it with the tenacity of a terrier.

This was ridiculous, she reprimanded herself. She was a grown woman. She should be coming home from a date to her own apartment, not sitting in her sister's driveway trying to figure out how to avoid a grilling.

The circumstances of her life had so far precluded living on her own. Six years of school, then the accident had made it easier to live with her parents.

Her temporary job here hardly made it worthwhile. She had thought of it before she moved, but Jenna had insisted and Rebecca didn't feel like bucking both her sister and her mother. When she moved back, then she would find her own place, she reasoned.

For now she had to find a way to convince her sister that nothing of import had happened today.

She pulled down the rearview mirror to look at herself. Her cheeks were flushed, and her eyes shone brightly.

Rebecca tried to frown, but couldn't. She couldn't suppress the happiness that threatened to bubble up and even now made her want to laugh out loud.

Joe Brewer and her? How had it happened?

She let her mind go over the day, recalling what they spoke of, what she had seen, what she had experienced. Not even with Kyle, whom she had so much more in common with, had she experienced such a feeling of oneness.

She stepped out of the car. As she walked up the graveled path, her feet crunching out an uneven rhythm, Rebecca forced herself to try to suppress the smile on her face. Forced herself to casually open the door and walk into her sister's house just as if she was coming back from a date with Dale.

Jenna was at the front door before Rebecca even closed it behind her. "So, where did you go?"

"I was out." Rebecca turned to face Jenna, smiling a more sedate smile. "The house was quiet, so I left."

Jenna nodded, wiping her hands on the dish towel she was holding. "Did you meet Dale somewhere?"

"I'll give you all the details later," Rebecca replied, evading the question. "I'm a little tired and I'd like to lie down for awhile."

"Sure." Jenna twisted the towel in her hands. "We'll be eating supper in about ten minutes. I thought we would wait for you."

"I won't need supper," Rebecca said quietly. "I'm going to have a shower and go to bed."

"Okay." Jenna frowned at Rebecca. "Are you sure you're okay?"

"I'm fine, Jenna. Just tired." Rebecca avoided Jenna's intense gaze and walked slowly past her sister. As she climbed the stairs to her bedroom and sanctuary, it was as if she could feel Jenna's disapproving eyes on her.

She had a shower and then, because she had to keep up the pretense, went to her bedroom, lying on the bed, staring at the ceiling.

It bothered her that she didn't have the nerve to come right out and tell Jenna where she had been. It made her feel disloyal to Joe, but she knew that once

Jenna discovered the truth, she wouldn't let off. And Rebecca didn't want to ruin the absolute perfection of the afternoon she had spent with Joe by listening to her sister's relentless criticism.

She turned her head to the cool breeze that luffed out her curtains, watching them almost hypnotized as she remembered Joe's words on the mountains, the easy way he spoke of God. She thought of her own attitude toward God, the resentment she had nurtured, the anger that kept her going.

Joe made it sound so easy. As if all she had to do was let go. But then what? Resign herself to walking crooked, to working the rest of her life in an office? Is that what God wanted of her?

She curled one hand under her head, her eyes absently following the motion of the soft fabric. Am I supposed to resign myself to being a cripple, God? she asked. Resign myself to working the rest of my life in an office? Is that what You want of me?

The combination of fresh air and good memories created a gentle lethargy that took the usual edge off her questions, and they became less demanding. I want to be whole. I want to go back a year. I want things to be different. Am I asking too much? Don't You promise that You will grant us the desires of our heart? She became panicky as she thought of letting go of the things she had held so close the past few months. She didn't know if she could do it. She looked away from the window as she forced herself to close her eyes, take a deep breath. Maybe I have the wrong desires. Maybe I need to change my focus, she thought as she slowly, one by one, listed all that she wanted and all she thought she needed. She set the list at God's feet. And her praying became a telling, not a convincing. She didn't feel as if she was prostrate, begging, pleading, repeating the same prayer.

It was, quite simply, a conversation. And as she felt herself relax, her prayers slowly brought sleep.

Jenna watched her sister make her way up the stairs and sighed. Rebecca never could fib with much conviction. A quick phone call this afternoon had told her that Rebecca wasn't with Dale. And Jenna knew that Rebecca would have told her had she gone anywhere with any of the women from work.

The bits of grass on her clothes and the distinct smell of horses were a dead giveaway. She had been with Joe Brewer. The fact that Rebecca hadn't told her showed Jenna she still had a chance to fix the horrible mistake her sister was going to make. A phone call to her parents was the start.

"Are you sure you want to do this?" Joe held Ben's bridle in one hand, his weight on one foot as he looked at Rebecca. She sat on the corral fence, holding the boards with a white-knuckled grip. She sat a few feet from where Mack stood ready, bridled and saddled.

Joe wasn't sure this was such a good idea. He had

no idea how bad her leg was and how riding would affect it, though she had assured him it would be fine.

Rebecca nodded once, quickly, as if she would change her mind. "As long as it's Ben I'm riding. You did say he was a quiet horse, didn't you?"

Joe nodded, hefting the bridle in one hand, considering. "He is. And I trust him completely. I just want to make sure that you do."

"I trust you, Joe Brewer."

Joe smiled at those words, at the affirmation in them. With a wink at her, he turned and slipped the bridle on Ben's lowered head. He buckled the chin strap and soon had the saddle on.

Joe flipped the cinch strap around and snugged it tight. He pulled on the saddle horn to make sure the saddle wouldn't slip, dropped the stirrups and walked Ben over to Rebecca.

"You know anything about neck reining?" Joe asked as he helped Rebecca off the fence.

"Not really." Rebecca laughed. She sounded self-conscious and nervous, and for the second time Joe wondered if he was doing the right thing.

"It's easier to explain once you're on the back of the horse," he said, dropping Ben's reins to the ground. Rebecca nodded and licked her lips.

"Okay," she said, sounding breathless, taking a step closer to Ben.

She looked small standing beside his horse. Joe lifted her on. Please behave, buddy, he thought. Be your usual gentle self. Once on the saddle, Rebecca drew in a long breath and blew it out, smiling tremulously at Joe. "Okay. I'm up here. Now what?"

"Put your feet in the stirrups," Joe said as he reached for the reins. Ben, bless his calm heart, stood perfectly still, his head slightly bent to allow Joe to slip the reins over his head. Joe handed them to Rebecca, absently giving Ben a pat on the neck.

Rebecca took them, and Joe explained the mechanics of neck reining. Joe knew once he got on Mack, Ben would obediently follow anyhow, but it was also important for Rebecca to feel she had some control over the horse.

He made her walk Ben around the yard, turning him in circles, getting her to make him stop and then go again. "Keep the reins loose," he called to her as she made another turn. "You just need a light touch."

Rebecca nodded, licking her lips. "This is a very large animal, you know."

"He's a stable horse."

"I hope that wasn't supposed to be a pun," she said, tossing him a glance.

Joe grinned as he caught her meaning. "Not a chance. I wouldn't inflict that kind of humor on my worst enemy."

Rebecca smiled at that, bringing Ben to a halt beside Joe. "So. How did I do?"

"You did just fine, Rebecca Stevenson. Just fine." He looked at her silhouetted against the sharp, blue sky and allowed himself a moment to appreciate what she had just done. He didn't know if he dared think it was for him but was thankful enough that she was willing to conquer her fear for her own sake. "You're quite something."

She blinked, her expression becoming serious as their gazes held. Time stilled, and it seemed as if the world had condensed to the two of them. She matters so much to me, Joe thought, resting his hand on her bent knee, wishing she wasn't so far up. He wanted to kiss her.

I love her.

He shook his head as the thought settled.

Yesterday, in the hills, away from everyone, it seemed easy to imagine the possibility, to indulge in the notion. But here, on his small place over the hill from his brother's ranch, it suddenly seemed more remote. Especially when juxtaposed against the sight of her in church beside her sister this morning.

He turned and looked around his yard, seeing the trailer and the self-built barns through her eyes. What did she think of him? Was he being foolish? Was he overshooting himself? What did he have to offer any woman, let alone one like Rebecca? And if he took over his father's ranch all he'd have was a run-down place and a pile of debts.

Joe took a step back, turned and walked slowly toward Mack, trying to make everything fit. Was he falling for her out of loneliness? Was he making more out of yesterday than he should have?

He caught Mack's reins, and one easy motion threw them over the horse's head. He stepped into the saddle. He glanced at Rebecca, who looked at him in puzzlement. In spite of his questions, Joe felt his heart lift as their eyes met once again. Maybe it would work.

"I guess we should get moving," he said suddenly, nudging Mack. He began walking, and Ben obediently fell in beside him.

The rhythmic footfalls of the horses were the only sounds in the warmth of the afternoon. As Joe stared ahead, he wanted to say something to Rebecca. But what?

I'm falling in love with you?

I need you?

And to what end? Wasn't the declaration or even the realization of it the beginning of a more serious relationship?

Joe couldn't stop his head from turning, his eyes from seeking hers. Just as he did so, she looked at him.

"Is something wrong?" Her delicately arched eyebrows were pulled together in a frown. "Am I doing something wrong?"

Joe shook his head, forcing himself to smile at her. "No. You're doing just fine."

She smiled at that, and Joe's heart once again forgot its rhythm.

"How long do you want to go for?" he asked, trying to keep the breathless note out of his voice. "Is Jenna expecting you back at a certain time?"

Rebecca shrugged carefully. "Not really. But I shouldn't stay away too long."

Joe picked up a hesitation in her voice. "Does Jenna know you're here?"

"Jenna is my sister, not my baby-sitter," Rebecca said quickly. "I don't need to tell her everything."

Joe said nothing in reply. It wasn't hard to figure out that Rebecca hadn't said anything to Jenna. The realization hurt. Was she ashamed of him?

Joe dismissed the thought as unworthy. He was spending too much time second-guessing this woman. He needed to trust her and to let go of his own hang-ups.

He kept to an easy trail, taking her over the hill toward his brother's place. The gates of the lower pasture were open, so he rode through them. The trail they were on would take them to a creek and some welcome shade.

Rebecca looked more relaxed. Her shoulders weren't curled, and she wasn't clinging to the reins. Once in awhile she would say something and Joe would reply, but their conversation was minimal. She was frowning in concentration that Joe didn't want to break, and Joe felt suddenly tongue-tied.

The air was utterly still. Not even a breath of wind disturbed the quiet of the afternoon. In spite of his T-shirt, Joe was sweating by the time they made it to the creek.

He got off Mack and tied him up, then turned to help Rebecca off Ben.

She sat in the saddle waiting for him, smiling hesitantly.

Joe reached up, caught her by the waist and easily lowered her to the ground. She reached up with a smile, catching her hands behind his head.

"That was wonderful, Joe." She shook her head as if she still couldn't quite believe it. "I haven't felt so free in a long time."

"Riding didn't bother your leg?"

"No. Not at all." She looked so pleased and proud of herself that Joe couldn't stop himself from dropping a kiss on her smiling mouth.

"I'm so glad you enjoyed it. It means so much to me."

"I know," she said quietly, tangling her fingers in his hair.

Show me what to do, Lord, Joe thought as he let her pull his head down for a kiss. I care for her more each time I see her.

Rebecca was the first to pull away, reaching to lightly touch his mouth. "What is happening, Joe?" she asked quietly, letting her fingers run down his neck and rest on his chest.

Joe shrugged, afraid to say what was on his mind, afraid to voice his concerns, afraid he might ruin the fragile mood.

"I guess we'll have to wait and see," he said, dropping a brief kiss on her nose. "Let's go sit by that tree."

She nodded, slowly walking alongside him. Joe

wondered if he should help her sit down or wait and see if she needed help. And he wondered why he felt like hitting himself on the head. He had never second-guessed his actions around a woman before. He was usually so self-assured. Now he was as hesitant as a teenager caught in the throes of his first crush.

Rebecca braced one hand against the tree and carefully lowered herself to the ground.

He caught her eye and they exchanged another smile. Joe wondered again where this would go. He didn't want to examine how much she meant to him. He only knew that with her beside him, he felt whole.

"Is this your brother's land?" Rebecca asked, leaning against the tree, the gurgling of the creek a hushed balance to the sighing of the pines.

"Yup. The creek misses the property I have by just a few feet." Joe leaned his elbow on his knee and looked through the pine trees to the sky above them. The pines swayed lightly in the wind, scattering the light.

"You're lucky, living out here," Rebecca said, her voice hushed. "There's so much space. A person feels free." She glanced at him. "I enjoyed riding, Joe. Thank you so much."

Joe turned to her and slipped his arm around her shoulders. His heart was full. "I'm glad you enjoyed it. You did well."

Rebecca laughed, lifted her delicate fingers to carefully brush his hair from his forehead. "All I did was sit on his back. I suspect a bale of hay would have done as good a job.''

''I think Ben enjoyed having you in the saddle more than a bale of hay.'' Joe pulled her close and kissed her again, her mouth warm and pliant under his. He felt again the need to have her near, to hold her. She felt right in his arms, under his heart.

Rebecca sighed, resting her head on his shoulder. ''Hard to imagine that all of this will belong to you,'' she said quietly.

Joe looked at the creek without seeing it, her words as cold as the water that flowed at their feet. The idea of ownership didn't give him the lift it should have.

Rebecca sensed his reticence and straightened, one hand resting on his arm. ''You're still not entirely comfortable with all of this, are you?''

''I don't know what to think.'' He pinched the bridge of his nose, not wanting to ruin the afternoon with thoughts of debt. ''It's going to be a lot of work and a lot of debt, and I'm not sure I'm up to either.''

''You're not afraid of hard work, are you?''

Joe turned his head so their eyes met. ''No,'' he said with firm conviction. ''I'm not afraid of hard work. I'm just afraid of hard work for nothing. I don't want to end up like my dad did.''

''Was it so bad?''

''What do you mean?''

''Not having a lot of money.'' She leaned forward, wrapping her arms around her knees, her head turned to him. She smiled carefully. ''I grew up with a lot of money, but that doesn't always buy happiness, either.''

''Maybe not. But it buys groceries. And while that doesn't always make a person happy, it's nice to go to bed with a full stomach and head off to school in decent clothes.''

''Were you that poor, Joe?''

Joe frowned, unable to keep his eyes off her, unwilling to show her a part of his life that had always been a source of shame to him. How would she understand? She who came from so much privilege? He looked away. ''We could never afford much. My dad was always scrambling for cash.'' He stopped. A shaft of anger pierced him as the memories came, unbidden.

''What about your mother? What happened to her?''

''Mom died when I was eight. Lane was six. Dad never really got over it.'' He felt Rebecca's hand on his knee and briefly resented her gesture of pity. But he let her keep it there because regardless of her motivation, it was a contact she had initiated. ''Unfortunately,'' Joe continued, ''he forgot that he had two sons and a place to keep up.'' He stopped again, aware of a complaining tone that had crept into his voice. He didn't want to go back to that. It was over.

''That must have been hard.'' Rebecca's hand tightened on his knee. Joe forced his mouth into a smile and looked at her.

''It was,'' he said simply. ''This place, in spite of

its beauty, doesn't hold a lot of fond memories for me. I lost a lot here, and I don't know if I'm ready to lose a whole lot more.''

''But you wouldn't Joe.'' Rebecca leaned closer, tucking her arm through his. ''I know you're worried about debt—''

''Not worried,'' he amended. ''Terrified. I look at the ranch and I see a huge, yawning hole that will suck everything out of me.''

''But it's a good investment, Joe.''

''Now you're talking like a banker.'' He tried to laugh, but couldn't. He didn't like what she was suggesting, the tone of the conversation. ''I've lived with debt, and it's no fun.'' And wasn't that the understatement of the year. No fun? It was gut-wrenching.

''Maybe part of the problem is how you see money. You have always been careful with it and that's good. But my dad always said that money is just a tool. I think that's how you have to start looking at it, Joe.''

''Easy to say when there's a lot of those tools lying around. It's a little bothersome when you're borrowing someone else's.'' He didn't mean to sound so harsh. Didn't mean his voice to take on that hard edge. But she truly didn't know what she was talking about.

''But the bank has faith in you, Joe, otherwise they wouldn't have even considered the offer.'' She caught his hand in hers and turned it over, touching each scar, each callus. ''You're a hardworking man, Joe. I hear that from so many people. I know you can do it.''

Joe felt it again. That all-too-familiar clutch of panic. The feeling that he was being pushed into responsibility, tied down to something he had been running away from since he left home. Poverty, shame, hard work with no reward.

"Money isn't as important as you make it out to be," she continued.

"It's not easy to live without it, Rebecca," Joe said, fighting to keep his tone even. "You've never had to do without. You've never had to work for anything."

He was sorry as soon as he said the words, and when she pulled away from him it confirmed his feelings that he had said the wrong thing.

"You don't know that much about me," she said.

"I know that you've grown up with more than I have." He struggled to find the right words to show her, make her understand. "I know that you have no idea what it is like to watch the sky, begging for rain to water the hay land, pasture and garden, knowing that without it, you would have to sell some cows, buy hay and food for the winter with money that you didn't have. I know that you haven't carefully peeled potatoes that had ten-inch sprouts growing out of them because that was all you had."

Joe leaned forward, his elbows on his knees, unable to look her in the eye, the memories coming too quickly, and with them shame and an anger he had never managed to get over. He tried to stop himself, but once started, he couldn't quit. "I wore rubber boots to school most of the time because they were cheaper and more versatile than running shoes. I can't remember a pair of blue jeans that weren't patched or shirts that weren't mended. Added to that were the failed tests because I had to help with haying or stay up the night before with a cow that was calving. I missed half of my classes trying to keep my father's ranch going." Joe couldn't help his rising anger. The disparity of the workload. Lane sneaking off to be with his friends while Joe, the sucker, stayed at home and worked like the little slave he was. "At thirteen I was training horses for other people to raise some ready cash. I owned my first pair of new pants when I was fifteen. When you were shopping around for your graduation car, I was selling my own horses to pay off a portion of my dad's debts. I'm sure if you knew me in junior high school, you would have looked the other way, I was such a skinny ragamuffin." He knew she would have been one of the girls who treated him with scorn, calling him a dumb farmer. Then he matured, his voice deepened, his chest filled out, and girls became willing to look past the clothes to what they thought of as a handsome young man. "Yes, it was very hard, Rebecca Stevenson. Someone like you will never know exactly how hard. You haven't had to work for everything you have."

Rebecca pulled away, straightening. She was quiet.

Joe avoided her gaze, staring ahead. She didn't understand, and he knew that in his struggle to show her, he had opened up a humiliating part of his life. He knew he shouldn't have gotten so angry, but he felt she had to know.

The silence became heavy, uncomfortable. Joe didn't know how to break it. She sat beside him, staring ahead, her back stiff.

"I...I should go," she said shortly.

Of course she should, he thought. She couldn't take the reality of his life. Besides, she was ashamed of him before she heard it all. Couldn't even tell her sister where she was. Joe shook his head. He was probably only a temporary diversion for a woman who had a temporary job in town.

Joe got up, brushing pine needles off his pants. Fine by him. Just as well he found out now as later.

Politeness made him hold out his hand to Rebecca, but she ignored it, getting up on her own. Without looking at him, she turned and walked to Ben, her steps hurried. Joe thought for sure she was going to fall, but she made it safely to the horses. He was about to help her on Ben, but she got on by herself. And he withdrew even more.

The ride to the ranch was quiet. Joe clung to his pride, the reliving of his past bringing its own peculiar pain. He had struggled so long with his resentment. He thought he had conquered it, but a few comments from Rebecca had shown him how fragile his victory had been.

Joe let Ben take the lead. They would have to unsaddle the horses. He was counting on that time to find a way to bridge the gulf that suddenly yawned between them. He prayed he would find the right words.

They turned the last corner and walked along the fence to his yard. Rebecca's head was bent, and Joe fought the urge to gallop beside her, pull her off the horse and beg her forgiveness, ask her not to judge him by a past he couldn't forget.

But he was held back by his angry shame and her sudden silence. A flash of silver caught his eye, and he turned. A big luxury car had pulled into the yard, and he wondered who it could be. Salesman, maybe.

Not that he cared. He had more important things on his mind right now.

He nudged Mack and came alongside Rebecca. He was dismayed to see the glint of tears on her cheeks.

"Rebecca, please..."

She wasn't looking at him. Her eyes were on the car parked in the yard.

Joe pulled up to the fence and jumped off Mack, then turned to help Rebecca off Ben. But she was already lifting one leg over the saddle, biting her lips in concentration. She lowered her foot to the ground, still clinging to the saddle.

As she tried to pull her other foot free, her weak leg gave way. She fell backward, her hands flailing, one foot still caught in the stirrup.

"Rebecca!" Joe called in fear. He couldn't move

fast enough to catch her. She landed heavily on her back. Ben took a step to one side, instinctively moving away from what he saw as a fallen rider, dragged Rebecca a step, then stopped.

Rebecca cried out, twisting her foot in the stirrup, panicking as she tried to free herself. Joe caught her foot, turned it slightly and eased it out. "Are you okay?" he demanded, dropping to her side.

"Yes," she said, her voice muffled behind hands pressed tightly to her face. Her chest was heaving, and she made no effort to get up.

Joe's heart leaped in his chest. He caught her shoulders, not knowing what to do, only knowing that he needed to make a connection with her.

"Your leg," Joe continued, frightened. "Did you hurt your leg?"

She drew in a loud, shaky breath, shook her head, but wouldn't lower her hands.

"Rebecca," he said more quietly, his hands touching hers, "please, look at me."

"Please," she pleaded, still holding her hands against her face. "Leave me alone."

"But Rebecca…"

"Just go away." She turned from him, curling into a tight ball. "Please just go away." In his peripheral vision he saw figures running, heard voices.

Joe crouched at her side, uncertain what to do, uncertain which event of this disastrous afternoon had caused this reaction.

"What happened?" A large man pushed himself

between Rebecca and Joe. Disregarding his suit, he kneeled in the dust beside Rebecca. "Baby, are you okay?"

Rebecca only nodded, still curled up, still silent.

"What happened, Roger? What happened to our girl?" A woman in a tailored suit rushed up and crouched, curving her hand around Rebecca's head. "How did she get on that horse? What is going on?" She looked at Joe, her eyes snapping. "Did you do this to her? How could you let this happen?"

Joe stood back, holding Ben's reins, holding the gaze of this obviously distraught woman. "I took her riding. She wanted to."

"What were you thinking about?" Jenna came forward, yelling at him.

"Don't you know anything of what has happened to her?" the older woman asked. She held his gaze, then her face crumpled. She looked at her daughter.

"Can you get up, Becks?" The man Joe guessed to be Rebecca's father gently pried her hands from her face. Rebecca allowed that. She slowly sat up, a large smear of dust on the back of her shirt.

"I want him to go away," Rebecca said, her voice low and fierce. "I don't want him to see me like this."

Joe felt his stomach lurch as he realized she was talking about him.

Roger Stevenson, kneeling by his daughter, looked over his shoulder at Joe, his eyes like flint. "You heard her. You had better leave."

Leave his own place? And go where? Joe held his gaze. "I'll bring my horses away," he said, his voice surprisingly steady. "What happened was an accident." And that was all he was going to say.

He gathered Ben's and Mack's reins and walked away.

Chapter Thirteen

Joe walked into the corral and glanced over his shoulder. Rebecca's mother and father were on either side of her. Jenna walked ahead of them.

Jenna opened the back door of the sedan, waited for Rebecca and her mother to get in then slammed the door.

As the car left in a cloud of dust, Jenna walked purposefully to where Joe stood.

Still stung at the treatment he had received on his own place, Joe turned away from her and tied up the horses.

"Joe Brewer," Jenna said as she came closer, "I need to talk to you."

"Then talk," he said succinctly.

Jenna looked taken aback, but only for a moment. "I'll wait until you're done with the horses," she said.

Joe was silent while he removed the saddles, brushed the horses and let them go. He brought the tack to the shed and returned. He brushed his hands off on his pants. Staying on his side of the fence, he leaned his elbows on it.

"So, what's on your mind, Jenna?" he asked, trying to keep his tone light and conversational.

"I'd like to know whatever possessed you to put Rebecca on the back of a horse."

"I thought it would help her conquer her fear." Joe squinted at Jenna, who stared at him, her face expressionless.

"Do you consider yourself a psychiatrist, Joe, as well as an impoverished rancher?"

Jenna was moving in quick and hard, Joe thought. He ignored her gibe. "I know she's afraid of horses and I know your sister wasn't willing to let it take over her life."

"So you thought you would help her?"

"She asked me to."

Jenna narrowed her eyes and shook her head. "I don't believe you."

Joe took a deep breath, praying for patience. He had lost his temper once already with disastrous results. He wasn't about to do it again. "Ask Rebecca your questions. She'll tell you."

"Rebecca doesn't tell me much."

"I gathered that. How did you know she was here?"

Jenna held his gaze, her eyes like Rebecca's and

yet not. They held an implacability and hardness that Rebecca's didn't. "When she came back yesterday with grass on her clothes and smelling like a horse, I took a lucky guess. She seemed ashamed to tell me that she'd been with you."

That one hurt, he thought.

"Do you have any idea what you're doing?" Jenna continued, her voice harsh.

"Why don't you just get to the point, Jenna?"

"Okay. Rebecca grew up with more money than you can imagine," Jenna said with a note of finality. "She's used to a higher standard of living than you could give her."

Joe blinked, hearing the venom in Jenna's voice as much as her words. "I know that, Jenna."

"I want you to leave her alone."

"That's up to Rebecca as much as me."

"Rebecca's had her heart broken already and has no defenses against someone like you."

"Someone like me? And what is that supposed to mean?" Joe straightened, struggling to keep his voice even. Coming so soon after his humiliating revelations to Rebecca, Jenna's statements hit too close to his shame.

"Joe," Jenna said, her voice taking on a patronizing tone, "we both know that you're good-looking. You attract women like honey attracts a bee. Rebecca has had very few boyfriends, and she's been hurt very badly by the one serious boyfriend she had."

"I know all about Kyle. And I know that he didn't

deserve her. Unlike Kyle, I see more than her physical appearance. And I like what I've learned about her.''

''You can like all you want. But what can you hope to give her? This?'' Jenna gestured around the yard, dismissing all Joe's hard work and scrimping with one contemptuous gesture. ''Can you see Rebecca living here or at that wreck of a place you used to live in?''

''I don't think you need to remind me of what I have and don't have, Jenna. But I do think it would be better if you let Rebecca make that decision.''

''You aren't getting it, Joe.'' Jenna took a careful breath, her arms crossed. ''Rebecca left my place on Saturday, and she didn't tell me where she was going. She left this morning after church, and the same thing happened. Don't you think that tells you something?''

It did, but only because it echoed Joe's misgivings about Rebecca's reticence.

''Joe, you saw the kind of car my parents drive. Had I lived any father from Calgary they would have taken their own private plane. Rebecca grew up in a house three times the size of mine. She has had everything she has ever wanted. She has never had to work for anything. Were they able to, my parents would have flown her anywhere around the world to a specialist to fix her leg. She doesn't have to work, but has chosen to for some reason my mother and I have never been able to figure out.'' Jenna stopped, taking a breath. ''I don't know what Rebecca sees in you except a novelty. I want you to leave her alone.''

"Rebecca means a lot to me—"

"I'm sure she does, given the differences in your bank accounts."

Joe sent out a prayer for patience and wisdom as he looked past Jenna to the hills beyond. "What I feel for Rebecca has nothing to do with how much money she has or how little I do. Don't think it hasn't been on my mind, as well, Jenna. I know exactly how much I have and what I can offer her." Joe looked at Jenna. "I think it is probably only fair to leave the decision up to Rebecca instead of either of us deciding for her."

Jenna blinked, as if surprised at his confession. "I would like to ask that you leave her alone for a while. I'm sure this little episode is going to bring back a lot of difficult memories."

"Rebecca and I have talked, as well." Joe's smile was bereft of joy. "I know about Kyle and the accident."

"And you still put her on that horse?"

"She wanted to," Joe repeated. He drew in a calming breath. The conversation had come full circle. "We don't have anything more to talk about, Jenna. If you do, you can call."

Jenna took a step back. "I might do that, Joe." She turned and walked toward Rebecca's truck, got in and drove away.

Joe pulled his hand over his face as Jenna's words echoed in his mind. As if he didn't know the differ-

ences between him and Rebecca. As if he needed to
be reminded of his lowly station in life. Again.

He walked to his trailer. He wanted to sit in the
cool shade, drink something cold and avoid thinking
about Rebecca and his future.

And he didn't even want to contemplate what her
parents and sister would be talking to her about.

Rebecca laid her head against the seat of her father's car, praying her mother wouldn't ask any questions. She didn't want to relive the humiliation of the
day.

She wasn't sure what events led to what. Only that,
in retrospect, she knew she was partially to blame for
the fiasco. She almost squirmed, thinking of Joe's
quiet question about Jenna's knowledge of where she
was. He hadn't said anything and didn't need to. Rebecca saw the hurt in his face. She had tried to save
herself some awkward questions from her sister, and
instead ended up looking ashamed of him.

"Are you sure you're okay, darling?" Delia's
voice was soft, concerned, and Rebecca turned her
head to her.

"I'm fine, Mother. I just overreacted."

"Did he try to do anything to you, hurt you in any
way?"

"No, Mother," Rebecca couldn't keep the anger
out of her voice. That someone should think that of
Joe!

"Well, we keep hearing that he's quite a flirt."

Delia folded her well-manicured hands in her lap, her tone gentle, but Rebecca heard the steel beneath the softly spoken comment.

"How do you keep hearing about him? I certainly haven't talked about him."

"We know that," her mother said pointedly. "But Jenna has."

Rebecca shook her head. Her family circled the wagons tightly whenever they perceived a threat, but this time they didn't realize that Rebecca had no intention of joining.

She sat up slowly, relieved to find that nothing hurt. Just her pride, she thought, recalling the humiliation of lying in the dust at Joe's feet. That's what happens when you get determined. She wished she could go back. Wished she could talk to Joe and tell him that she didn't care about his past. Tell him how she really felt about him. But she had let his anger determine her actions and spur her pride. The result had been humiliation.

"Joe is a good friend who has helped me a lot the past few weeks." Rebecca looked directly at her mother. "This isn't the first time we were riding." Okay, technically the last time she wasn't really riding. She had been as frightened as she'd ever been, but some spark of mischief urged her to prick her mother's rigid hauteur.

Delia's eyes widened, and she turned to her husband, who was driving. "Roger," she said. "Did you hear that?"

Her father caught her gaze in the rearview mirror. "Are you sure that you should?"

Rebecca nodded, holding her father's regard. "I enjoy it, Dad. I enjoy it more than I ever thought I could. And I never felt afraid. Not with Joe. He has such a connection with his horses. It's a God-given gift."

Roger Stevenson smiled at that. "You sound quite excited about this man."

"I am." Rebecca sat up, surprised at her declaration but even more surprised at her father's smile. "Yes, I am. I've been waiting for someone just like him."

Her mother blanched. "Honey, Jenna said all he's got is a tiny wreck of a trailer and no business whatsoever." She lifted her hands to her daughter, pleading. "Rebecca, you sound so starry-eyed over this young man, and I know why. It's a romanticism and mystique that surrounds horses. Then there was that movie that came out last year. He's just a novelty for you. And you know what happens with novelties."

"What do you mean by that, Mother?" Rebecca asked, stung by the easy way her mother brushed aside feelings that Rebecca knew she had never had for anyone before.

"Rebecca." Delia's voice took on that mother tone that never failed to annoy for the simple reason that Delia often brought up things Rebecca didn't want to face. "Remember that short-lived fling you had with painting?" she asked, her perfectly plucked brows lifted with just the right degree of condescension.

"That lasted three months. And what about dancing? Or your skiing lessons and the music lessons? All short-lived. You haven't finished much—"

"Most of these hobbies were your idea, not mine."

"You couldn't even stick it out with your therapist in Calgary," Delia continued, as if she hadn't heard.

Rebecca clamped her mouth shut, stemming the tide of explanations that would only make her mother feel right.

"Besides, Jenna said he's quite the ladies' man."

"Joe happens to be a man, not a ladies' man. He's honorable and kind—"

"And dirt poor." Delia shook her head, her mouth thinning. "Not our kind of people."

Rebecca heard her mother's words, an echo of what Jenna had said not too long ago, and her anger flared. "I don't want you to say that about him. Joe is a sincere Christian, an honest, caring and gentle person." She stopped, unwilling to voice feelings that were still so fresh and untried.

"Roger." Delia appealed to her husband, her voice rising. "This has got to stop."

Roger Stevenson said nothing as he turned into Jenna's driveway and turned off the car.

"Did you hear me, Roger? She has got to see reason."

Roger turned in his seat and looked at his daughter. "I trust Rebecca to make decisions that are right and true. I think after all she's been through, she should know better than anyone what is best for her." He winked at Rebecca, and she was momentarily stunned. Then she smiled at her father, thankful for his support.

"You can't be serious, Roger." Delia opened the door, her mouth turned up in distaste. "You've always spoiled the girl rotten. This isn't some trinket she wants that you can give her. If she gets tired of this, she can't throw it away or quit." With those words, Delia strode up the walk, her silk scarf fluttering behind her.

Rebecca got out of the car, her mother's words hooking their barbs in her. She knew she had received much as a child and had many opportunities to try different things. But she had finished the things that mattered to her. She had a physical education degree because it was the only thing she had truly wanted.

Until she met Joe.

In spite of the differences in upbringing and in spite of what her mother and sister perceived as a lack, Rebecca knew that Joe had much to offer her.

But after what had happened this afternoon, she wasn't sure he'd want to see her again.

Her father was waiting for her. He held out his arm, and she took it with a wan smile.

As they went up the walk, Jenna pulled into the driveway. She must have been right behind them, thought Rebecca with relief. She didn't want to imagine what Jenna would have said to Joe had she taken the time to stop to talk to him.

"I'd like to go up to my room," Rebecca told her

father as they entered the house. "I don't really feel like facing Mom and Jenna at the same time."

"You can't avoid it, honey," her father replied, patting her hand awkwardly.

"I know, Daddy. But I just want to be alone for a while." She was afraid to face the double-barreled threat of her mother and sister after what had happened at Joe's place. She knew she would cry if she did. And the last thing she wanted was to show weakness in front of them.

She walked wearily to her bedroom. Disregarding the dust on her clothes, she dropped on the bed. Images flashed through her mind, snatches of conversation as she relived the afternoon with its undertones of mistrust and anger.

She wished she could call Joe and fix what had been broken. He had been angry. She knew, looking back, she had been naive. But the memory of herself lying in the dust at his feet kept intervening. It was too humiliating to think that he had seen her like that. It was too visible a reminder of how disabled she was. Couldn't even perform the simple task of getting off a horse.

Rebecca dropped her arm over her eyes. *I wish I could go back and do today over again, Lord,* she prayed. *I like Joe. I like him a lot, and I don't know how to tell him because I don't know how he feels about me.*

Rebecca stopped, waiting. She remembered the service this morning, the songs they sang and how, for the first time in a while, they had begun to speak to her. How she had allowed herself to be lost in adoration of God, who had made the wonderful places Joe had shown her. How she had realized that all she had from her youth, the faith she had been raised with, was still there. She only needed to allow God to penetrate other parts of her life on His terms, not hers.

Joe had shown her what she needed to do. He had been a strength and example for her.

And after this afternoon, she didn't know where their relationship was going.

She would just have to leave it in God's hands.

"Can I come in?"

Jenna's voice at the door made Rebecca sigh. She didn't have the emotional reserves to deal with her sister right now. But this was Jenna's house, and if she didn't catch her now, she would later.

Rebecca got up and opened the door, and Jenna walked in, followed by her mother. Reinforcements. Rebecca walked to the bed and sank down on it.

"I don't want to talk about Joe." Rebecca looked from her sister to her mother, deciding to save them the trouble by getting right to the point.

"Fine." Delia settled on the delicate wooden chair beside Rebecca's bed and crossed her legs, carefully arranging the drape of her pants. "Then we'll talk about why you thought it unimportant to tell Jenna where you were going."

"I don't believe this." Rebecca shook her head,

leaning on her hands as she tried to stare down her mother and sister. "I'm not fifteen. I don't think it's necessary to discuss everywhere I go and everything I do."

"You are living in Jenna's home. It's called manners, Rebecca," her mother chided.

Rebecca forced herself not to feel like a chastened teenager. "I'll concede the politeness part, but I don't expect Jenna to tell me where she's going."

Delia merely pressed her lips together at that.

Jenna leaned forward. The second part of the tag team. "Rebecca, you've got to understand that as far as Joe is concerned I only—"

"—have my best interests at heart." Rebecca finished the sentence for her. "You should hear yourself, Jenna. You're so predictable. What does putting down Joe have to do with my best interests?"

"You're taking care of his banking files. You know exactly what he has."

And I know even better than you did what he grew up with, she added to herself. Rebecca pressed her lips together as she remembered what Joe had told her about his childhood. What he had revealed before she left in a huff.

Even now she could hear the pain in his voice when he spoke about his past. She wondered what it had cost him to tell her.

"Joe is a good person…" She stopped, hearing the lameness of the words. "He's a sincere Christian."

"No one is debating that point," Delia said condescendingly. "I'm sure at heart he's a decent fellow. He's just not for you."

"Why not, Mother?"

Delia tilted her head and shook it lightly as if she couldn't understand her daughter. "Rebecca. You have traveled the world. You have spent more money in a single shopping spree than I'm sure he has in an entire year. I understand he's very good-looking, and I'm sure that has its own appeal. But good looks fade, and then what will you have?"

Rebecca was stung at her mother's assessment of her. "Do you really think I'm that shallow, Mother?"

"Of course not," Delia said hastily. "I wasn't implying that. You're caught up with a fantasy right now, but reality is much, much different. You have never had to struggle on your own. You can't begin to understand how difficult it is to make ends meet."

"And don't forget," Jenna broke in, "that Joe has had so many girlfriends. I'm sure he just sees you as another fling."

Rebecca didn't want to touch that one. It struck too close to her insecurity. The one thing she couldn't get past. Her disability, limp, problem—call it what she would, it made her feel less womanly around Joe. But she couldn't sit and let her mother and sister put down a man who had given her so much. "Joe is one of the most honest and giving men I have met. I've learned a lot from him."

Rebecca saw Jenna give her mother a sidelong glance and was sure they wished she was twelve again and could be banished to her room. But she wasn't twelve. She was twenty-five. And most women of twenty-five were living on their own. As she should be, she thought with sudden clarity. If she was tired of feeling smothered by a well-meaning sister and mother, then it was up to her to do something about it.

Jenna sighed. "Well, Rebecca, I wish I knew what to tell you to change your mind. I just don't want to see you hurt."

"I know you don't, Jenna. And I appreciate it. I appreciate all you have done for me. You're a giving, caring sister. But I'm wondering if maybe you've been doing too much."

"What do you mean by that?"

Rebecca slowly breathed in, the idea so fresh she wondered if she even dared voice it. But she knew she must, or she would lose heart in front of the formidable forces of her sister and mother. If she wanted to be independent, there was only one person who could do that for her—Rebecca herself. "I'm thinking I should move out," she said boldly.

Jenna frowned. "Move out? What are you talking about?"

"Move into my own place. Rent an apartment. Be on my own." As soon as she spoke the thought, she felt a clench of fear. She'd never been on her own. Had never had to fend for herself in any way.

"Don't be ridiculous," Delia said curtly. "You don't have the first clue how to take care of yourself.

You've never even had to buy groceries. You've never had to make those kinds of decisions. You've never had to work for anything.''

Her mother's words echoed Joe's, and that, more than anything, gave her the courage to hold out. "I've had to work for a number of things, Mother," Rebecca said, calm pervading her. "I've just never had to make those day-to-day decisions. But I'm a quick learner."

"And what would you furnish this apartment with?" Jenna sat back, shaking her head. "You don't have anything."

Rebecca laughed. "I work at a bank. I know better than most people how easy it is to borrow money."

Jenna dismissed the idea with a wave of her hand. "You'll change your mind in a couple of days." She got up. "Are you going to come downstairs for supper or stay up here and sulk?"

Rebecca ignored her sister's comment. It was a no-win question. Jenna left, quietly closing the door.

Delia got up, her face suddenly crumpling. "Rebecca, honey. I sense that you care for this young man. And that's good. But..." She lifted her hands as if in surrender. "It's one thing to spend time with someone like him, but it's quite another to encourage him when you know this relationship can go nowhere. You don't know what it is like to scrimp and watch every penny. Do you think your father was born rich? He had to work for everything he has."

"But you married him anyway, didn't you," Rebecca pointed out triumphantly.

Delia closed her eyes as if praying for patience. "It was very difficult. You don't know how difficult." She opened her eyes and stared intently at Rebecca. "I made those sacrifices so my daughters wouldn't have to."

Rebecca looked at her mother and smiled. "You made your own choices, Mother. Let me make mine."

"You're a very stubborn girl, Rebecca Stevenson." Delia shook her head. "You're just like your father."

"Then I should do just fine, shouldn't I?"

Chapter Fourteen

"Are you sure you'll be okay, honey?" Roger Stevenson hesitated in the cramped hallway of Rebecca's new apartment, looking around him with a frown. "You'll be all alone."

"I'll be fine, Daddy." Rebecca leaned against the wall, taking some of the strain off her leg. She was bone weary, and her leg ached from getting up and down to unpack boxes. But she knew if either of her parents found out, they would fuss. "I sure appreciate all your help, though."

"Gladly given, dear." Roger leaned closer to his daughter, his hand on her shoulder. "Your mother will get over this, as will Jenna," he whispered. "Just give them time."

Rebecca smiled and, giving into an impulse, gave her father a quick hug. He hugged her awkwardly.

"Thanks again, Dad. For everything." She swallowed, pulling away. "You've been great about all this."

"Have you gone through this apartment with the landlord?" Delia called from the bathroom. "I hope he knows that there's a crack in this mirror."

"He knows," Rebecca called down the hall. "He told me he's getting a new one."

Delia came out of the bathroom, spreading lotion on her hands. "Knowing landlords, I doubt he will," she said succinctly. She glanced once more around the living room, frowning. "This room is definitely an improvement."

The apricot-colored couch and chair were brand new, as was the glass-topped coffee table. The television and stereo came from her parents, and Jenna gave Rebecca her old kitchen suite. A few generic prints hung on the wall. As an added touch, Delia had brought a set of candlesticks that sat on the coffee table. It looked cozy and welcoming.

"Are you done, Jenna?" Delia called over her shoulder, studiously avoiding Rebecca's eye.

Still ticked with me, thought Rebecca.

Delia and Jenna had spent the better part of Monday trying to get Rebecca to change her mind. In vain they pointed out the economics of being on her own, the cost of setting up an apartment. "It's hardly necessary. Why, it's only for six months, darling." When that failed, they decided to humor her, hoping she would give up. But Rebecca wasn't swayed by their antagonism or their condescension. Fortunately, Wakely's vacancy rate was high, and she quickly found a decent apartment.

Jenna and Delia were reluctant accomplices, donating their castoffs, helping her buy what she needed, arranging for a mover.

Roger Stevenson had quietly done what he was supposed to do—used his money and influence to speed a few things up and in general provided Rebecca with much-needed emotional support. A couple of times Delia and Jenna almost convinced Rebecca to stop the process, to keep things going the way they were.

But memories of what Joe had said, the parts of his past that he had shown her made Rebecca realize that if she was ever to understand Joe, to forge some kind of bond with him, then she had to show him that she didn't need her parents or their wealth. It seemed a feeble and futile effort, but she knew that she had to at least try. Besides, she needed to keep busy, to dull the hurt of the trust that had been broken Sunday afternoon.

"There. Your bed is all ready for your first night alone." Jenna came out of the bedroom, casting a critical eye over the living area of the apartment. A few items still lay on the wooden table tucked away in one corner of the living room, but the rest was ready.

"Thanks, Jenna. Mom." Rebecca held out her hands to her mother. Delia raised her eyes heavenward, as if questioning her part in this move, but then folded Rebecca in her arms.

"You're welcome, dear." Delia pulled away, her hands on her daughter's shoulders, a forced smile pulling up her mouth. "I just hope you don't regret this."

"I won't. I think it's high time I lived on my own."

"But, darling..." Delia sighed, waving her hand in a futile gesture. "Never mind. I guess when you come back to Calgary, we'll have to figure out what you're going to do."

Rebecca swallowed a knot of pain. She didn't want to think about moving back to Calgary. She didn't want to think that far ahead. Didn't want to think that she might be leaving Wakely. And Joe.

She hadn't talked to Joe since Sunday. She'd jumped each time the phone rang, but he hadn't tried to call her at Jenna's place or the bank.

She was too ashamed to call him, too aware of what had happened the last time she was with him.

Rebecca tried to push the pain aside. "We'll see what happens in the next six months," she said.

Jenna tossed her an enigmatic look. "What will happen?"

Rebecca said nothing as Jenna's words drove the sorrow deeper.

"I'm done," Jenna said, turning to her parents. "I should get back to the girls." She reached over and patted Rebecca on the shoulder, avoiding any other contact. "Well, kiddo. Hope it goes good. Call me when your phone is hooked up."

"I'll do that. Maybe I'll have you, Troy and the girls over for supper one night," Rebecca said, forcing a light tone into her voice.

"Sure," Jenna said quickly. "Mom, Dad, I'll see you at home, then." And with that Jenna walked out of Rebecca's new apartment.

Delia sighed and faced her youngest daughter. "You'll be okay?"

Rebecca felt a moment's trepidation. "Yes," she said with finality. "I'll be fine. This is Wakely, not downtown Chicago."

Delia raised her plucked eyebrows a fraction, glancing out the window of the basement suite. "At least downtown Chicago has apartments with elevators," she said dryly.

"Like Jenna said, call us when your phone is hooked up." Roger gave her a quick hug, and as he did, Rebecca felt him slip something into her back pocket.

Trust her father, she thought, hugging him tightly. They pulled apart, and Roger winked at her. "You'll do okay, Rebecca. I'm sure of it."

They smiled at each other, then as Rebecca held the door, her parents left. Rebecca waved to them as they walked down the hall, their goodbyes echoing down its long emptiness.

When they disappeared around the corner to the

stairs, Rebecca closed the door and leaned against it. The silence of her apartment closed in on her.

She drew in a deep breath and walked slowly to her stereo, all hooked up and ready to go. She needed music to ease the silence. She flipped through her CD collection, then pulled out a collection of cello concertos by Vivaldi.

"Slightly melancholy, with a promise of joy," she said as she put it on. "Perfect for the girl living on her own for the first time in her life." And perfect for a woman who was heartsore and lonely.

Rebecca dropped onto the couch as the first strains of music drifted through the air. She laid her head back and breathed slowly, stilling a momentary flash of panic. She'd been alone before, she reminded herself. As a teenager she'd often been on her own while her parents were gone for the night. But that was her home, where she grew up. Not this strange new place with its unfamiliar smells and sounds.

Rebecca let the haunting sounds of the cello flow through her and forced herself to relax. She closed her eyes as a lump formed in her throat.

Joe. She couldn't stop thinking about him, couldn't erase his image from her mind.

She wanted to see him, yet was afraid to. Yesterday she worked up enough courage to call him, but only got the answering machine and hung up. Even the impersonal tone of his voice on a tape was enough to start her hands shaking and her heart pounding. It was so easy to conjure up his image in her mind. His grin, the way his hair fell across his forehead, the soft murmur of his voice as he assured her and encouraged her.

Too easily, she remembered his arms around her, his strength and his gentleness. His conviction and his faith.

Oh, Lord, she prayed, I really like him. I love him. I don't know what to do. Show me what to do.

She didn't want to think about him, didn't want to remember what had been lost. Didn't want to think of might-have-beens. But she couldn't stop. She lifted her head and looked around.

She got up and walked slowly around the apartment as if discovering it for the first time. Jenna's old wooden table sat in one corner of the rectangular living room across from the small kitchen. Some books were on the table, and Rebecca idly picked them up. An old educational psychology textbook, an accounting textbook, a few dog-eared novels.

Her Bible.

Rebecca's hand lingered on it, and she smiled wryly. She lifted the book and paged absently through it. Words, long familiar, slipped past her roving eyes, phrases from her youth. Still skimming, she slid into a chair and set the Bible on the table.

She slowed as she came to the Psalms, always her favorite readings. She knew some of them by heart, and skipped those that spoke of tribulation and death to enemies. She was looking for comfort.

"I will say of the Lord, 'He is my refuge and my

fortress, my God, in whom I trust.'" Rebecca smiled as she read. "He will cover you with His feathers, and under His wings you will find refuge. His faithfulness will be your shield and rampart."

Solid words, comforting words. She drew them close to her, closing her eyes as she slowly opened her soul, drawing on the comfort offered her in the psalm. She reached out, seeking God's comfort, His strength. She felt alone and, for a brief moment, afraid. But as she opened her heart, she felt His nearness, His comfort, and her heart lifted in thankfulness.

She read until it was dark, her thirsty soul drinking up the living water of God's word.

Joe swung the hammer once more, and the nail head sunk into the wood. He straightened and wiped his forehead with his bandanna. It was unseasonably warm, and he prayed it wasn't an indication of what the summer was going to be like.

It wasn't the only thing he had prayed for, he thought as he dropped the nails he held into the cracked leather carpenter's pouch he wore low on his hips. He had tried to keep busy, to keep thoughts of last Sunday out of his mind. But like any bad memory, they would come back in unguarded moments, tormenting him and replaying over and over.

Why had he gotten so angry at Rebecca's gentle, probing questions? She was only trying to get to know him, and in true Brewer fashion his pride got in the way, and in true Brewer fashion he had over-reacted.

Joe dropped his hammer in its metal bracket on the other side of the pouch and bent to lift another board.

He had talked to Dale on Monday. Rebecca wasn't in. Dale had told him he was fairly sure the loan would go through and to go ahead on the improvements Joe wanted to do. So each day since Sunday, he had worked hard at the home place in a futile effort to rid himself of the memories, to expiate the past. Lane had moved out on Tuesday, leaving only a brief note for his brother. He would contact him when he was settled.

It made going to the ranch easier, knowing that he finally had it to himself.

Each day after work, he would saddle Ben or Mack and head out to check the cows and calves, letting the land work its wonder on him.

In the hills, away from work, from the house, he would find the peace that eluded him. In the hills he could let go of pride, put his troubles in the context of eternity and allow God to heal his battered heart.

By Wednesday he had finished the corrals and rebuilt most of the fences. He had done some work in the arena. A few of the stalls were still intact. Others had been stripped for their lumber. It would take about a month of work before he could move his horses in. It wasn't as spacious and roomy as the arena he had hoped to build, but it was workable.

With each board he put up, each repair, he kindled

the glimmer of hope he had hardly dared allow himself when he started. He could make this place work. Haying season would be busy, as would calving, but he could carve out sufficient time to work with his horses and make a living from the ranch. In time, with hard work and thrift, he could build up his training clientele.

In spite of his optimism, however, evenings meant coming home to his small trailer. Stephanie had called a couple of times about another horse trip. Kristine had phoned, sounding contrite.

But from Rebecca, nothing personal. He thought of her message on the answering machine the other day. Her soft voice, spelling out the details of his loan, should it go through, gave him an unwelcome jolt.

Joe wondered why he had put himself through this, put his hopes for the future in the hands of a young woman who grew up with so much. Ever since he had quit school he sought situations that put him in charge of his life.

Now he was poised on the brink of this dark valley of debt. He had started on this path with the hope that he would be able to realize his dreams. Then he had dared to entertain the idea that he might have something he could give Rebecca. But Jenna's comments wormed their way past his self-esteem, digging up his own history and humiliating memories.

Sunday had been a disaster, and he didn't know how to go about fixing it. Rebecca obviously didn't want to see him or hear from him.

Maybe Jenna was right. Maybe he was just a novelty to Rebecca. Now that she was found out, embarrassed in front of her family, the novelty had worn off.

His thoughts went from hope to frustration. From the ranch that began to seem more hopeful each day to Rebecca, who seemed further and further out of his reach.

Joe set one end of the board on the ground, then walked to the other end to nail it down. This was the last one. He bent over, set the nail against the wood and with a few good hits had it anchored. He hoped work would do what it usually did, keep his mind from turning over things he couldn't change. He had prayed, had let go, had tried to figure out what God wanted. But he was tired of the second-guessing he had been indulging in all week, and was weary of wondering and thinking.

He knew one thing. Regardless of what happened, regardless of who Rebecca was, he cared for her in a way he never had for another woman. He loved her.

Joe hit the nail again, letting the words settle in his mind, allowing himself to acknowledge the feeling.

And what are you going to do about it? he thought, nailing the board. He stood, pushing his hand in the small of his back, easing out the kink.

He was done here. He had nothing to do except wait. Wait to hear if the loan went through. Wait to see what Rebecca was going to do. And pray.

He had done enough of both, he thought, pulling

off his carpenter's pouch. He looked at the mountains that hovered, eternal and solid. His problems were no more than a leaf in the wind compared to their solidity and age.

He was tired of waiting, thinking and wondering. He hadn't heard from Rebecca, but he hadn't called her, either.

He made a sudden decision.

I've got nothing to lose, Lord. He sent out another prayer for wisdom, strength. Then he turned on his heel, strode from the corrals, skirted the arena and dropped his pouch into the back of his truck.

He stepped into the truck and with spinning tires headed into town. He didn't even stop at his own place for fear he would change his mind.

The whole drive to town, his prayers kept the mocking thoughts at bay. He was a child of God, as was Rebecca. That was enough.

He pulled into the bank's parking lot, looking for Rebecca's vehicle, but he didn't see it. Taking a deep breath, praying as he did so, he pushed open the door and walked into the bank.

Sharla looked at him, her eyes wide.

Joe looked at his dirty shirt, the rips in the knees of his jeans, suddenly aware of the bandanna that held his unruly hair down. He didn't care. Not anymore.

"Is Rebecca in?" he said gruffly.

Sharla shook her head, then glanced down. "She's, um, not in. I mean not right now."

Joe's heart plunged. What if she was with Dale, the

guy who had everything? He didn't want to think about it, couldn't. Joe leaned on the desk, his face inches from Sharla's. He tilted his head, forced a smile, hoping the old charm would help him out now. "Then where is she, Sharla?"

She leaned close to him, her eyes shining. "I'm not supposed to tell anybody, but she's at the hospital right now."

"What happened?" Joe straightened, fear knifing through him.

"Nothing." Sharla frowned. "She goes there three times a week."

Joe relaxed. Of course. Therapy sessions. She had talked about them once. Briefly. "Thanks, Sharla. You're a doll." He winked at her, turned and left.

He lost no time going to the hospital. He found an empty spot, parked the truck and waited a moment, his fingers tapping restlessly on the steering wheel, second thoughts finally finding the time to plague him.

He pushed open the door and got out. He focused on memories of Rebecca in his arms, Rebecca smiling at him. He clung to them as he pushed open the door of the hospital.

Taking a deep breath for courage, he walked to the reception desk. "Can you tell me where the physiotherapy department is?"

A nurse looked at him over her half-glasses. She took in his torn jeans, the bandanna on his head, censuring them with one condemning glance, then pointed down the hall. "Follow the green line, stop when it stops." That was all she said, looking at her computer screen.

Great welcome person, thought Joe. He pulled his bandanna off, finger-combed his hair in an attempt to settle it.

Joe walked down the hall, the heels of his cowboy boots echoing on the hard floor. The hallway made a turn then unexpectedly opened up into a large area. Mats lay on the floor. To his right a man puffed away on an exercise bike. Directly in front of him a person dressed in casual clothes was holding a toy just out of reach of a young boy. Against a wall, walking on a stationary treadmill, was Rebecca.

Joe stopped, swallowing at the sight.

Rebecca's soft hair was darkened with sweat, her eyes shut tight as she clutched the rail in front of her. Her yellow T-shirt had a triangle of sweat across her shoulders and down her back. Her steps were halting but steady. It wasn't hard to see, however, the intense concentration, the deliberateness of her movements.

He leaned against the wall, suddenly seeing another part of her. A part he was sure she wouldn't want to reveal to him. But he couldn't stop watching. He suddenly remembered his comment to her that fateful afternoon—you've never had to work for anything—and once again he was ashamed.

The treadmill was slowly increasing in speed, and he could see it was getting more difficult for her to maintain her momentum. She stumbled, and Joe straightened, ready to run over.

But a physiotherapist was at her side, quietly speaking to her. Joe could see her shake her head quickly, her eyes still closed. The therapist stepped back but kept her eye on Rebecca while she went to another patient.

Joe worked his way around the room, unable to stay away, unable to keep his eyes off the slight figure working so desperately hard.

He was behind her when she stumbled again. This time she didn't regain her balance. The relentless motion of the treadmill dragged her leg away. She struggled to pull it back. The therapist had her head turned.

Joe could see that she wasn't going to make it. Her hand slipped.

The therapist turned her head and jumped up.

But Joe was right there. He caught her from behind, easily plucking her off the machine.

She collapsed against him, panting, heat radiating from her body.

Joe held her close, rocking her gently as her hands clutched his shirt, his heart pounding.

"What are you doing here?" she gasped, her head bent.

Joe held her. He could feel her muscles trembling, could feel her heart's heavy pounding. "I'm sorry, Rebecca, but I'm not going to let you go."

She struggled, then slowly relaxed against him. "Joe, I didn't want you to see me like this, didn't..."

She looked at him, her face flushed, her eyes shimmering with unshed tears. "Joe, I'm sorry."

"For what?" He gently pushed a damp strand of hair from her forehead, looking for an excuse to touch her.

"For Sunday. I was wrong."

"You did nothing wrong," he whispered. "I was wrong to get so angry. I was ashamed, too. But I had to see you, had to tell you…" He cupped her cheek, tilting her head to look at him. "I love you."

Her eyes opened wide, and her mouth fell open. "What did you say?" she asked, breathless.

Joe caressed the corner of her mouth with his thumb, ignoring the stares of the people around them. Slowly he lowered his head and touched his lips to hers.

One hand clutched his shirt, the other held his neck. He couldn't hold her close enough, couldn't seem to absorb the reality that she was in his arms, that she was returning his embrace.

He tucked her head under his and continued to hold her, rocking her gently. He didn't know what to say, didn't know how to tell her that what he had just seen had shown him ever more clearly that he wasn't going to let her go. Not now.

Or ever.

Rebecca stood in the bathroom, her hand on her heart, leaning against the countertop. Joe was here. Joe had come for her! In front of a room full of people, he had told her he loved her. Rebecca could hardly absorb it. He had seen her at her most vulnerable, had held her tightly in his arms. He loved her. Her heart sang.

She turned, looking in the mirror, touching her lips as if to find the evidence of his kiss there. Then, with a grin at her reflection, she turned and almost floated out of the room.

Joe waited in the reception area, his elbows resting on his knees, his clasped hands dangling between them. He was staring into space, a light smile teasing his well-shaped lips. Rebecca stopped to watch him, allowing herself a moment of pure joy. This wonderful man was waiting for her.

This wonderful man loved her. And she loved him.

He turned his head, caught sight of her and got quickly to his feet. Unconsciously he ran a hand over his hair, trying to straighten it. His expression became serious as he watched her.

Rebecca touched her hair, then taking a steadying breath, she walked slowly to him.

"Hi, Joe." She stopped in front of him, still unable to make that first move, her self-consciousness still holding her.

"Hi, Rebecca." He slid a hand in his back pocket, shifting his weight to one foot. He tilted his head, slowly reached out and ran a rough finger along her cheek.

She reached up and caught his hand, turning her mouth to press a kiss against his palm.

He gathered her close. His lips touched hers, a contact as light and ethereal as gossamer.

Her breath stopped as she reached up to steady herself, her hand coming to rest on the warmth of his chest.

He said nothing, only slipped his other hand around her waist, drawing her closer to him, as he increased the pressure on her mouth, deepening the kiss.

Rebecca rested against him. Was this her being held so close, being kissed so tenderly by this man so many women wanted?

She shut her thoughts off, held in his embrace, his mouth moving gently over hers. She clutched his shoulders, returning his kiss.

Joe moved his mouth to her cheeks, her forehead, then laid her head in the curve of his neck, resting his chin on her head. He sighed once, his chest lifting beneath her cheek, his arms still holding her close.

Rebecca kept her eyes closed, as if to shut out the world, to reduce it to Joe's arms around her, hers around him. Together. His chest lifted in a sigh, his arms holding her, his chin resting on her head.

"I had to see you," he said finally. "I couldn't stay away."

"Don't say anything. Please." Her voice was muffled against his shirt. "It doesn't matter." Being held close to him changed everything.

"I meant what I said, Rebecca. I love you," he whispered against her hair, holding her tightly. "I don't have much to offer you."

Rebecca drew back, knowing better than ever what it cost him to say that. "You have as much to offer me as my father had to offer my mother," she said, smiling at him. "My dad wasn't always rich. I didn't know that. My mother just told me the other day."

Joe smiled crookedly. "I do have a place for us, small as it may be."

"We're only the two of us, Joe." She linked her hands behind his neck, enjoying the right to do so, emboldened by what he had told her. "I don't need that much room."

"But you're used to so much more."

"Of course I am. I didn't choose to have a lot of material possessions, any more than you chose to have little. But I trust God to help me learn."

Joe shook his head, his hands tightening on her waist. "You're quite a woman, Rebecca Stevenson. I don't deserve you."

"Joe," she whispered, her voice suddenly thick with emotion. "Please don't talk like that. It has nothing to do with deserving or not deserving. I love you. You have given me so much." Her voice broke, and she laid her head against the warmth of his chest, absorbing his strength, his love. Thank You, Lord, she prayed, I'm the one that doesn't deserve him, but I thank You.

A cart rattled by, and from a speaker above them a disembodied voice paged a doctor.

Rebecca quickly wiped her tears away and straightened. "We should get out of here," she said, looking around. The hospital was empty this time of the day. "I need to have a shower."

"So do I," he said with a rueful look at his dirty clothes.

Rebecca took his arm, and together they walked outside.

"I'd offer my place, but it wouldn't be right."

"I don't imagine Jenna would appreciate having some dirty farmer in her shower," Joe said with a laugh, slipping his arm around her shoulder, shortening his pace to hers.

She glanced at him. "I've got my own place now."

Joe stopped, frowning at her. "What do you mean?"

"I'm not living with Jenna and Troy anymore. As of Monday, I've been living in my own apartment." It felt so good to tell him that.

"Really?" Joe smiled, toying with her hair, his other hand resting on her shoulder. "Why did you do that?"

"I thought it was time to be out on my own. Past time, probably." She bit her lip, wondering how her next statement would sound. "I guess I didn't want you to think of me as a spoiled little rich girl who always had everything handed to her."

"I'm sorry," he said, his voice contrite. "I never meant—"

"I know what you meant and didn't mean, Joe. But you were right when you said that I didn't know what it was like to support myself. I've never had to make it on my own. I've never had to make any major decisions. I want to be worthy of you, Joe. I want to show you that I can take care of a house, that I can live with less." She stopped, unsure how to tell him. Opening up to him was still new for her.

"Oh, Rebecca." It was only two words, but in those words she heard approbation, humor and, even better, love. His quick hug sealed it.

"I've got my own vehicle here," she said softly. "If you want, you can come to my place in a couple of hours, and I can make you supper."

Joe winked at her, the simple action sending a quiver of pleasure through her. "You got a deal."

Joe smoothed his hair, took a quick breath, switched the flowers he was holding to his other hand and hit the button beside Rebecca Stevenson's name. When her voice came over the intercom she sounded as breathless as he felt.

"Come on in, Joe," she said. The buzzer sounded, and Joe opened the door, then ran quickly down the steps to the lower level. He strode down the hall, hoping quick movements would quell his nervousness, the red carpet muffling his footsteps. She hadn't chosen the best apartment in Wakely, he thought, noticing the burn marks on the carpet, the scuff marks on the wall. She really wanted to show him that she could live with less.

He found her apartment and lifted his hand to knock on the door, but it opened before he hit it.

Rebecca stood in the doorway, smiling at him, her eyes shining, her copper-colored dress catching the bronze highlights in her hair. "Hi," she said simply, standing aside to let Joe come in.

He handed her the flowers he had bought before he stepped inside, and she took them with a smile. They hesitated, a couple discovering each other, uncomfortable together yet unable to stay apart.

"Go in the living room and make yourself at home. I just have a couple of things to do before we eat."

Joe nodded, suddenly reticent. She closed the door behind him, and he walked into the apartment.

It was simply furnished, yet little touches showed him that this was a home. Candles in holders on the coffee table, a dried flower arrangement on an end table, pictures on the walls. A book lay open on the couch. The small table in the corner was set for two. It looked cozy and inviting. Joe looked around, smiling. "I like your place, Rebecca."

"I like it, too," she said from the kitchen. She set the bouquet on the kitchen table and came up beside him, her hands clasped. "I'm really enjoying being on my own." She looked positively smug, and Joe had to laugh.

"How long are you planning on living here?" he asked.

She was quiet, looking at her hands, her thumbs pressed together. "Until my job is finished, or..." She glanced at him, then away. "Something else comes up."

Joe was quiet. What they spoke of wasn't the same as what they discussed in the hospital. The conversation was headed in the wrong direction.

But he clung to the memory of her in his arms this afternoon, what they talked about then. He cleared his throat, determined to get any second thoughts and doubts out in the open. He swallowed as he turned to her, taking her hands in his, struggling once again to find the right words, words that would convince her. "Rebecca, I love you." Basic words, true words. Not very original, though, he thought, looking at her beautiful face. She deserves so much more. Please, Lord, he prayed, show me what to say, give me strength to say it. He cleared his throat as his heart began to race. His words would open him to her. "Rebecca, I've never cared for anyone like I've cared for you. I want to marry you. Like I said before, I don't have a lot to give you. I can't promise you that we'll never have problems. But I know that with God's help we can do it. I know that."

"Please don't define who you are by what you have." She bit her lip, her eyes shimmering with tears. "I hope you think more of me than that."

"I think a lot of you, Rebecca. Too much," he said with a short laugh.

Rebecca smiled, then reached up to touch his face, her fingers soft and cool. "I love you, too, Joe," she whispered. "I want to be your wife. I want to marry you."

Joe blinked as her words registered. Then he gathered her close, his seeking mouth found hers, and they sealed their words with a kiss.

He felt himself relax, felt a weight drifting off his shoulders. His soul mate, his life's partner. Rebecca.

Rebecca was the first to pull away, her head lifting slowly, reluctantly. "I smell my supper," she said.

Joe nodded, reluctant to let her go. He held her arm loosely, letting her hand slip through his as she walked backward to the kitchen. "I should go and put it on the table."

"Sure," he said, still holding her fingers. She gave them a gentle tug, and with a grin, he released her.

In a few minutes they were sitting at the table. Joe held out his hand to Rebecca, and without hesitation she laid hers in his. He closed his hand over hers, squeezing it lightly.

"Will you ask a blessing, Joe?" she said quietly.

Joe nodded, his heart full to overflowing. A last look, and then they bowed their heads.

United in prayer.

United in a love divine.

Epilogue

"Stay here, honey." Rebecca held her daughter's hand tightly and shifted her son, Paul, to her good hip. "Mommy has to say goodbye to Daddy."

"What the men doing onna roof?" Katie pointed to the new building about twenty feet away, looking at her mother.

"They're putting on the shingles. That will keep the rain off us when we move into the new house." Rebecca squinted against the sun, watching the men on the roof. One figure straightened, then waved.

Rebecca let go of Katie's hand long enough to wave back, smiling at the sight of her husband without his shirt, his bronzed back gleaming with sweat. He walked slowly along the roof then clambered quickly down the ladder.

He jogged over, reaching to pick up his daughter and swing her in the air. She squealed with delight.

Joe leaned forward and pressed a quick kiss to Rebecca's mouth. He tasted salty, he smelled of sweat and tar, but his nearness still made Rebecca's heart skip. "Come down to boss us around?" he asked, setting Katie down.

"I just thought I would say goodbye. I'm off to the school," Rebecca said with a grin, reaching out to wipe a dark smear off her husband's forehead. "The house is looking great."

Joe glanced over his shoulder and nodded, his hands resting on his hips. "At the rate we're going we should be all settled in before Christmas. Should be able to squeeze your family in for Christmas dinner."

"I'm sure they'll be suitably impressed at both your speed and your talents," Rebecca said with a smile, rocking Paul.

Joe winked at her. "Think Jenna will, even though it doesn't have a solarium and formal dining room?"

Rebecca shook her head. Joe was always trying to push Jenna's buttons and was constantly teasing her about the missing solarium, which Jenna still dreamed and talked of.

"You going now, coach?" he asked, glancing over her track pants and T-shirt.

Rebecca nodded. "I'm bringing the kids to Jenna's. There's a casserole in the oven if you get hungry before I come home. I told the girls that if they won the last volleyball tournament they could have a shorter practice, so I might be home earlier."

Joe grinned at her. "Keep this winning streak up and you'll have to start charging the school for your volunteer coaching time."

Rebecca swung Paul on her hip, her smile smug. "That might happen anyway. Mr. Kowalchuk offered me a part-time position teaching phys ed next year."

Joe stared at her, then he grabbed her and Paul in a hard hug. "That's great." He whooped. "Just great." He blew out a breath and wiped his forehead with his bandanna. "My wife," he said proudly.

"You look hot," Rebecca said, feeling sorry for him. She was going to spend the rest of the afternoon in an air-conditioned gym while he would be working out here in the hot sun.

"It's just pretty warm out today."

"This is great weather for building, but I sure wish it would rain." Rebecca glanced at the pasture, a twinge of worry flitting through her.

Joe rubbed the light frown away from between her eyebrows. "We've managed so far," he said, reaching to pull her close, Paul hanging between them. "Our lives are in God's hands. One way or the other, we'll get by."

Joe took the baby from her, curving his arm around her waist.

"Then I guess I don't have to worry, either, do I?" said Rebecca, leaning against him.

As they held each other, they looked across the land toward the mountains that stood, unchanging, through the ups and downs of their lives. It was a daily reminder of God's love. Unchanging, solid, ever the same.

It was enough.

*   *   *   *   *

Dear Reader,

I have *Matthew* 6:25-36 printed out on a piece of paper sitting by my computer as a reminder to me of what I should be expending my energy on. Worry has been a struggle for me as long as I can remember. I have worried about stains, world peace, our ranch, forest fires and my children's faith. Each day, in various ways, God brings me back to His word and His comfort.

Don't worry. Trust in Me.

Joe and Rebecca both had to learn the same lesson, but each of them learned it in their own way. As we all do.

Don't worry. Trust in God.

Carolyne Aarsen

P.S. Please feel free to write me. Send letters and comments to: Carolyne Aarsen, Box 114, Neerlandia, Alberta, Canada T0G 1R0.